Harbour View

To Marg,
With my best wishes –

Harbour View

Binnie Brennan

QUATTRO BOOKS

Canada Council   Conseil des Arts
for the Arts   du Canada

We acknowledge the support of the Canada Council for the Arts
which last year invested $20.1 million in writing and publishing throughout Canada.

Cover art: Binnie Brennan
Author's photograph: Kathy MacCulloch
Cover design: Diane Mascherin

Library and Archives Canada Cataloguing in Publication

Brennan, Binnie,
    Harbour view / Binnie Brennan.
ISBN 978-0-9810186-4-5
    I. Title.
PS8603.R461H37 2009   C813'.6   C2009-904239-8

Published by Quattro Books
P.O. Box 53031, Royal Orchard Postal Station
10 Royal Orchard Blvd., Thornhill, ON L3T 3C0
www.quattrobooks.ca

Printed in Canada

For my parents,
Mary Lou and Geoffrey Payzant
And for Tim

One's life should always be read twice, once for experience,
then once again for astonishment.

— Wayson Choy

One

The sound of trickling water enters his dreams, interrupting the jig that is playing itself over and over, unfinished. It is never finished, and exists nowhere but in his mind, culled from a thousand fiddle tunes he has played in his lifetime. Jigs, reels, strathspey fragments; all his life they have kept him company. Sometimes laments. But the water is real, and the sound of it is wakening him.

Partly in sleep, Buddy does a quick inventory, first a minute stretching of fingers and toes, then a straightening of his legs and arms, just enough to generate an inner creaking without bringing on the aches of his age. Spring water rushes down the side of a mountain as the ligaments groan in his neck, replacing the fiddle tune. Now that he is fully awake, the rushing water is caught in the acoustic of his bathroom. Once again, a plumber will need to fix the toilet.

The sun warms his face, touches the hollows where his eyes once were. Buddy knows it is winter, and he enjoys the irony of the sun's warmth through his window. The harbour might well be filled with warships moored and awaiting designation, ferries zig-zagging between and around them, bringing cars and their drivers from one shore to the other. But he knows this is no longer so; he knows a bridge spans the near-empty harbour, bearing cars from Dartmouth to Halifax. A few containers and tugs will make their way through the water, and maybe some sailboats, even at this time of year. Buddy knows it all, but he prefers to remember things otherwise. For this his blindness is a blessing.

"Good morning, Buddy! What a bee-*yoo*-tiful day it is out there. The sun's shining and the icicles are beginning to melt. How'd you sleep last night? Get your beauty rest? Today's your big day, you know."

Lord save us, that Nurse Muriel's a talker. But Buddy likes the smile in her voice, the brightness she always brings him even when he is tired, which is nearly always, now. He holds out his stiffened fingers for her to wipe with her cool cloth, enjoys the softness of the towel she hands him. Presses it to his face and breathes its laundered dryness.

"That toilet of yours running again? I'll call Maintenance, have it fixed up in a jiff." Bed sheets rustle as Nurse Muriel tidies his bed. "Time to change your pants, I'd say. Lemme go find Sam."

Pants. Trousers, the King would say. And they're really not pants she's talking about. Not even underpants, but something worn underneath, something to catch the drip. Buddy reaches for his belt buckle. It is not there. Even if it were, his fingers couldn't do anything about it. His hands rarely do his bidding any more.

Buddy draws a breath, air which carries with it the scent of antiseptic, of old age. And of something else, warm and comforting: chicken casserole, his favourite. Salt and starch, just as Mavis used to make, the peas soft and undemanding.

There is a tap at the door.

"Hi there, Buddy. Let me give you a hand."

Sam speaks softly, unlike Muriel and the others who are trained to speak so the deaf may hear them. Sam's quiet is a relief, like the silence when an aircraft engine cuts out: you don't really notice the racket until it's over.

The door creaks and settles in its frame.

"Did you sleep well last night?"

Buddy nods and opens his mouth to speak. His words will emerge in a stale-smelling cloud, but Sam seems not to mind.

"I slept like a baby. Dreamed of..." Buddy must pause for breath. "... of fishing in my grandfather's dory. Beautiful vessel. She could chop through waves as high as..." His arm travels upward, finishing his thought. "*Beatrice II*, she was called."

"Was she named for someone?" Sam's hands are moving quickly, cleaning and drying. Buddy hardly notices.

"Named for..." Another breath. "... for Grampa's mother, my great-grandmother. She was a red-haired beauty with a fearful temper. Afraid of nothing and no-one."

"Just like the dory."

"Just like the dory, yes. Never once capsized."

"The dory or your great-grandmother?"

Both men chuckle. Sam has finished his job, Buddy knows from the snap as the younger man pulls off his gloves. The tap water runs and Sam's hands slurp together, lubricated by soap from the wall pump.

"Special day for you today, Buddy," echoes his voice from the bathroom. Buddy frowns, trying to think why. "Cook's preparing your favourite. Chicken casserole."

పౕ

There is a burning patch of skin at the back of his head, enough to nearly waken him. Buddy turns his head to ease the pressure of the chair back against his skull. The sound of rain dripping from trees interrupts the music that haunts him always when he sleeps, fiddle tunes both vague and precise.

So many years later, at this level of near-wakefulness, Buddy still tries to open his eyes. Maybe this time he will see the morning light dappled against the blue floral wallpaper, the movement of his wife's lace curtains in the breeze. Before he can remember that there is nothing at all to see, the discreet click of his door being pulled shut awakens him fully. Buddy sits up straight.

The quiet is anticipatory. Even the trickle of the toilet seems muted. Buddy holds his breath, waits for the sound of the gurney rattling by in the hallway. Soon his door will be opened, and one of the staff may or may not greet him. Closing his door is a habit of theirs; they sometimes forget that what he cannot see, he can hear.

Mrs. Nickerson, bless her soul, the words drift quietly to him from the hallway.

Again there has been a death, and again it is not his own.

He is the oldest person here at Harbourview Centre, this he remembers from his last birthday. There was chocolate cake, and Cook prepared his favourite meal, chicken casserole.

Buddy's thoughts tumble into place like the gears of a clock. Today is his birthday. That's why the air is filled with Cook's salty casserole. And that's what Nurse Muriel and Sam meant by today being his special day. He has had one hundred and eight birthdays before this one. Which means this is his one hundred and ninth. Lord save us.

Buddy reaches for the radio on the table to his left. A stiff finger presses against the knob, and his room is filled with the sweeping sounds of a full orchestra over which soars the voice of a lone violin. It pulls him back to the Cape Breton Highlands, the spruce-covered mountains, cliffs sweeping down to the water. Rocks along the shore holding the scent of the sea, of fish, dark water cold enough to make your calves ache just looking at it.

"Buddy?"

He has not heard the door opening.

"Buddy, dear, it's time for lunch. Let's get you ready." Nurse Muriel's voice grates as she hums, off-key, "Happy Birthday." Buddy presses the knob and abruptly the music is gone. He hopes he has not winced.

"How about one of your bow ties? Something special for your birthday. Which one would you like? There's a green one for Saint Paddy's Day, a black one for dressing up, and oh my, here's the Nova Scotia Tartan. How about that? Nice and festive-like."

Buddy nods his assent, and Muriel places the tie in his hands. He lifts his collar with shaking hands and slides the tie around his neck. Makes the first turn before his fingers fail him. As Muriel finishes the job, her hands, so close to his face, exude a familiar sweetness.

"My wife used to wear a perfume just like that," he says.

"My heavens, really? It's hand lotion. She must've used the same brand. Vaseline, I think. Well, I'm glad you like it! Come on, then, dear. I'll help you into your chair."

When Nurse Muriel wheels him into the dining room there is a sudden hush in conversation, a cessation of cutlery clattering against plates. A single, droning voice continues, something about the weather. Must be one of the deaf ones, Buddy thinks. Sam's voice, unusually strident, cuts through.

"One-two-three, Happy Birthday to you…."

His baritone, strong and sure, carries the elderly, warbling voices along in a well-meant rendering of the daft tune. Buddy smiles, and at the end of it he puts his dry hands together to make a papery sound, not quite clapping. There is a speech from the Harbour View Centre's director, congratulating Neil-Duncan "Buddy" MacDonald on his birthday as though it's a great accomplishment. "We wish you many more, Buddy!" Muriel squawks from the back of the dining hall. Buddy smiles and shakes his head, no. No more; this is enough for him.

There is the sound of a violin tuning, and the sudden joy of a strathspey splashes over him. Buddy puts one hand to his heart, and conducts with the other. He'd know that caramel sound anywhere; it's the fiddle from his youth. Alice must have come to surprise him.

After lunch Cook wheels out a cake, overly sweet, and ginger ale to toast the birthday boy, as Nurse Muriel insists on calling him. And then he is tired. Sam wheels him back to his room and helps him to his bed.

"I didn't know you had any other name but Buddy," Sam says as he plumps the pillow.

"Neil-Duncan, all one word. The firstborn son of the firstborn son in my family is…" Buddy pauses for breath. "…is always given that name. It was my father's name, and my grandfather's. But they called me Buddy as a child, not to confuse me with my Da and my Grampa."

"What about your grandson?" Sam asks.

"Trouble is my son only had daughters. But my daughter had a boy she named for me. Keeps the tradition going."

"Any other family traditions?" Sam pulls the mohair blanket over top of Buddy.

"Yes, there's the fiddle. Duncan MacDonald, my great-grandfather, made a fiddle that's been passed down along with the name. Firstborn son of the firstborn son is taught to play from a wee lad, and when he marries he is given it. It's quite unusual, carved with a thistle crown instead of a scroll. You'll have heard it today at lunch."

There is a silence.

"Heard what, Buddy?" Sam's voice is careful.

"Heard the fiddle. The very one with the thistle crown. My daughter, Alice, was playing a strathspey."

"Ah, Buddy? Maybe that was something you heard on the radio earlier today."

"You must have stepped out when she was playing, Sam. It was marvellous! You missed the step-dancing, too, then."

"I guess I did, Buddy. Listen, have a good rest, and then maybe later you can tell me more."

"All right, Sam. Thank you."

The rushing water amplifies, but Buddy does not mind. In some ways it is a comfort. He feels his eyes close, another illusion, as the warmth of sleep drifts over him. His feet twitch as the strathspey rings through his dreams of red curls and dancing feet.

᧞

A man can outlive his wife. It's a harsh fact of life, but one you can live with after a fashion. A man shouldn't outlive his children, though. But Buddy has done so. He has outlived them all.

Miraculously, his boys were spared their lives during the War. Morris, the youngest, died ten years ago of cancer. Neil-Duncan, the eldest, died not long before that, of old age. Of all things, old age. Lord save us.

And the Lord did save us. But only some of us.

The hours before the explosion that took his eyes are never far from his thoughts. The laughter, the scent of meat cooking outdoors, the sunlight reaching through the canopy of leaves, these are the easy memories. Even in the shade, Mavis wore a hat, the better not to freckle. She never did accept that her freckles were the first thing that caught his eye all those years before, and she was convinced that wherever she was, the sunlight would catch her. Their daughter, Alice, on the other hand, sought the sun's warmth, lay on the grass away from the trees with her arms spread out in welcome.

The impossible memories, those buried deep, wait until sleep claims him. Only then is he granted his final seeing moments: a smiling Alice unscrews the cap and then tips the tin towards the fading coals. The arc of golden liquid holds the light her mother always shunned, suspended for a small eternity while Mavis reaches, screaming, "No, dear, no…."

The taste of butane sometimes invades the back of his throat as Buddy wakes up coughing and weeping tearlessly, brimming with the unanswerable *why*.

❧

It was the loss of Alice, the middle child, which created in him a great, gaping void. Taken far too young, leaving her husband broken and her small boy bewildered, his daughter's death all but destroyed Buddy.

It is the sound of her that he has most grieved. Alice's voice, pure as the highland air, brought fresh tears every time Buddy heard her sing. And her fiddle-playing was unmatched, both in sweetness and in vigour. Once warmed up she'd be twirling and kicking while the bow danced on the string, her red hair bouncing against her shoulders in time to the jigs and reels that poured out of her and through the fiddle, filling the air with pure, unbridled joy. She was like the devil possessed, others used to whisper. But to Buddy there was nothing devilish about her; she had the face and the voice of an angel. Hers was a God-given talent, one which he'd longed for as a young man and had given himself to wholly when he saw it in his daughter. He would watch her with prickling eyes while one of his boys banged at the piano and the other picked at the guitar. By the time the boys' voices had dropped, they were working in the pits, bringing home cash and coal dust, more interested in weekend gambling than the ceilidhs. It was Alice who kept the fiddle singing.

ༀ

"Did you learn to play on it?"

Sam is pulling Buddy's socks off, buttoning his pajamas.

"Oh yes, my Da taught me. I used to put on quite a show. In the early days Mavis and I were asked to play at the kitchen parties, you know. She played a wonderful piano. Taught our children, she did, and I showed 'em how to play the fiddle. But you know…" Buddy breathes deeply, "You know, Great-Grandpapa Duncan's first-born never did play on it. He wasn't right, never grew any larger than a five-year-old."

"Really?" Sam settles into Buddy's creaking chair. Buddy pauses. It's been a long time since anyone cared to hear his stories. His descendants wear them as they do their elbows, as something that's always been there and is scarcely to be noticed. Buddy coughs into his handkerchief, then continues.

"Story was Duncan carried him around in a basket strapped to his back. And when William, the other son, was big enough, he did it too. The three of them would go off fishing in the dory together, William rowing, Duncan fiddling and singing, and Neil in his basket."

"So the traditions began with William."

"Yes. It was William who named his boy Neil-Duncan, and passed along the fiddle to him."

"Where's the fiddle now, Buddy?"

Buddy brings a hand to his chin and ponders. One of his grandchildren must have it, or maybe a great-grandchild.

"I believe my boy Neil passed it to his daughter, or perhaps it was his grand-daughter. Jennifer, I think. She wasn't interested. Shame, isn't it? Such a beautiful instrument."

He remembers the fiddle from when he could see, knows it like the back of his hand. It was the colour of honey, beautifully carved, not a wayward line anywhere. And it wasn't only the delicate thistle crown that set it apart from other fiddles; it was its voice, soaring and full one minute, fine as a whisper the next. That voice rendered the air holy, caused grown men to weep and babies to quieten. The fiddle was created by a master, laden with his soul. Duncan never made another; it was the last one.

"He apprenticed with his father, Duncan did. Learned all he knew about carving from him. He brought…" Buddy must breathe. "He brought one over from Scotland, but it was ruined when he washed up on the shore."

"Washed up on the shore? Who…? Buddy, you sure about that?"

Buddy wheezes his amusement.

"Sure as the day is long, Sam. He jumped ship and barely made it to shore. Beatrice saved him, you know. She found him among the rocks and nursed him back to health. Then they married."

Sam's silence amuses Buddy. He can imagine his mouth hanging open, his head shaking in disbelief. Perhaps his own family has not handed down the treasures of their past to him.

"Have you any family traditions, Sam?"

"Nothing as rich as yours, Buddy. I'm named for my uncle, and my ancestors came over from Ireland during the Potato Famine. That's all I really know. That, and my uncle Seamus spent time in jail for tax evasion. Pretty exciting stuff, eh?"

"Don't you sometimes wonder what drove your ancestors to leave their homeland?"

"I guess they must have been pretty hungry. Food was scarce. Everyone was leaving Ireland."

Buddy sighs. "I never did learn what put my great-grandfather, Duncan, on the sailing ship from Scotland with nothing more than the fiddle strapped to his back. That's one detail I've always wondered about."

"Maybe there are some things we're not meant to know," Sam says slowly. "Or we're better off not knowing."

"Do you really believe that, Sam?"

Sam's generous laugh fills Buddy's room.

"Neil-Duncan MacDonald, maybe that's your secret to a long life. You're full of optimism."

"Always, Sam. Always."

❧

"Buddy, oh, *Bud*-dy! There's someone special here to see you."

Nurse Muriel opens his door, and before he can ask who it is, she's bustled in some strangers. Perfume makes its way to him, nothing familiar.

"Grandpapa? It's me, Jennifer. Alice's grand-daughter."

"Alice?" Buddy straightens and catches his breath. Her voice sounds older, somehow rusted. "Sweetheart, is that you?"

"No, no, it's Alice's grand-daughter, Jennifer. I've brought my son with me, Buddy Junior. He's named for you. Remember when he was a baby?"

Buddy exhales slowly. He smiles and nods, although he does not remember. Of course she is not Alice, this stranger who knows him. Alice is long gone. There are now too many descendants and too few visits and no way of keeping them all straight. Buddy has never smelled this woman before in his life.

"We're in Halifax for a few days. Dad told me it was your birthday, so we just had to come see you."

"And where have you come from, Jennifer?"

"Oh. Right. We live in Toronto. Buddy Junior is here on a university tour."

"Lord save us, university. What will you study, boy?"

Buddy turns his head to where the young man might be standing.

"I'm a musician. I'm thinking of auditioning at Dalhousie."

The boy's voice is deep, as his own once was.

"Do you sing, boy?"

"Buddy Junior sings and dances, and you'll never guess what he plays, Grandpapa!"

"Mum..."

"You'll just be so proud!"

"Mum!"

The boy's voice is pained, exasperated. Buddy wonders if he is tall or short.

"Sorry, dear. You go ahead and tell him. Better yet, why not play something for him?"

Buddy waits. There are familiar sounds of latches flipping, of things being picked up, put down, and picked up again. Fingers brushing against strings, checking the tuning: E-A-D-G, as recognizable to him as the sound of his own voice. And then the room is filled with the sounds of his early days. Buddy settles back in his chair and listens, allows the reel to course over and through him. He is grateful that his tears may not flow, grateful to these strangers who are his own descendants as he is Duncan's, and who have brought the sound of heaven to him, early.

"Buddy's had a big day." Nurse Muriel's voice is, for once, gentle, as the warmth of a blanket surrounds him. Nothing can interrupt this particular performance.

"Is he asleep, or...." The woman's voice is hushed.

"He sleeps a lot these days. Who wouldn't, at his age?"

"I guess your playing put him to sleep, Bud. You'd better pack it up. We should go."

In his mind's eye a foam of red hair tumbles to Alice's shoulders. She prances around his room with the blue floral wallpaper as her backdrop, laughing and fiddling like an angel. When she leaps out the window and over the harbour, Buddy opens his eyes wide and stares.

Two

She will never get used to the smell of this place. The combination of antiseptic and soiled diapers is awful enough, but what upsets her the most is the starchy odour of institutional cooking which hangs in the air like a putrid, yellow fog. Even after six months, Dahlia finds herself suppressing her gag reflex, especially at mealtimes. Yesterday noon it was chicken casserole. Yet again, a plate of mush dotted with dead-looking peas. Can't they ever get the peas right?

And who will help her with her socks?

Dahlia leans forward, yesterday's sock in hand (or is it from the day before, she forgets). Her stiff back and the recliner get the better of her, and she sits back with a whoosh of an exhale. Can't even see her own feet! Her rounded belly and purple-veined legs, encased as they are in elasticized trousers are now her enemies, conspirators in pain and clumsiness.

There was a time when they glided her around on the ice until her nose was frostbitten and her toes numb with cold. Dahlia can practically taste the hardboiled eggs, two in each pocket, supplied by her mother on skating days. Up at first light, Dahlia was off with her skates, sailing over the frozen Dartmouth Lakes until dusk. There was nothing better than a golden egg yolk on an empty stomach, washed down with a mitt-full of snow.

It appalls her that she can no longer pull on her own socks.

੨

Who will help her today? Better not be that awful Muriel, with the singsong voice and the rough hands. Or Stella, whose fierce and shiny black face frightens her. Much as Dahlia hates being dirty, she hates her bath more, being manhandled into the tub, prodded and scrubbed by uncaring hands. She will go without this week, and no-one will notice.

Last week she splurged on a pedicure, dipping into what savings she is permitted. Fixed income, indeed. There's nothing "fixed" about one hundred dollars a month the government allows her, now that they have clawed back everything so she may live here. Bingo earnings and the monthly stipend can be too easily swallowed up on cigarettes, shampoo, and new socks and underwear that have a way of disappearing with the laundry. Now that Ronnie is gone, she has no-one reliable to pick these things up cheaply at Wal-Mart, so she mostly does without, even if it means begging the odd cigarette from one of the staff workers. She never asks the other women, perched in rows on the benches in their dung-coloured coats, lips collapsed around their own cigarettes and avoiding her gaze.

So what if she ends up wearing the same pair of socks for a few days in a row?

Oh, she can just hear Ronnie: "Dale, I never thought I'd see the day you'd wear dirty socks. What's gotten into you, Old Woman?"

The edges of her mouth turn up, in spite of herself. Ronnie called her that from the beginning, *Old Woman*. And now it's true, she is an old woman, she thinks, easing her head back against the chair.

"Morning, Miss Dahlia!"

Oh good, it's Sam, what a relief. He's the kind one, the only one who doesn't talk to her like she's a child. With a flourish, Sam places her plate on the table next to her. "Another gourmet delight!"

Dahlia sniffs. On the plate sit two triangles of white bread glued together with tinned meat, and a dried-out pickle on the side, ripple-cut, as though that might make a difference.

"You gotta eat it, Miss Dee, or I'm in big trouble. You too, remember? You had an insulin shot, and your body needs a little something mid-morning. You don't want to fall down like you did last month, do you?" Sam's eyebrows furrow at the sight of the sock dangling in her hand. "Say, isn't this your bath day?"

"No, no, I had my bath yesterday," Dahlia lies. "Sam, won't you help me with my socks?" She holds them out to him.

Sam's smile is sympathetic as he hunkers down to ease the socks over her puffy feet. At least he's gentle, and he compliments her on her painted toenails.

༒

The first time Ronnie touched her feet, Dahlia was nearly paralyzed, so overcome was she by guilt, lust, and confusion. Ronnie had slowly unlaced her skates, eased them off and enveloped her frozen feet in large, capable hands.

"You don't want them warming up too fast, or they'll hurt. Let me rub them a while, then we'll put them in some water." Eyes the colour of frozen ponds held her gaze for longer than she could bear. "What you doing without woolen socks, anyways? You're gonna be walking like an old woman."

Dahlia simply nodded, and allowed Ronnie to minister her feet. When she could stand again, she leaned against Ronnie, glad of a strong arm to help her home. Undone by those enormous grey-blue eyes. She knew then she'd never be the same, that her life would never be easy.

༒

"What's that you're saying about woolen socks, Miss Dee?"

Startled, Dahlia sees that it's Sam before her, not Ronnie. Her heart thumps a warning. Careful, she thinks.

"Never you mind, I'll see if I can find you some slippers to warm up your feet."

Sam pulls open a drawer, and fishes around before pulling out her ratty old bedsocks, so worn in the heels you could spit through them. Dahlia rests her chin on her fist and stares at the top of his head while he slides them on over her socks. His close-cut hair is thinning, encircling his shiny crown like the first feathers of a duckling. It must be soft to the touch, Dahlia thinks, with a longing that surprises her.

"You okay, Miss Dee?"

His words land quietly, filling her with sudden warmth. Dahlia nods and looks at the floor. If she looks up at his kind face, she will cry.

"I gotta go help Missus Cuthbert next door, but I'll come back real soon, okay? Here, let me unwrap your sandwich."

Dahlia says nothing, but to please him, she picks up the soggy white bread and moves it toward her mouth. Sam waves on his way out the door, and Dahlia drops the sandwich into the wastebasket by her chair.

ॐ

"Good morning, Dahlia!"

Dahlia is startled from her sleep. Her neck jerks forward off the back of the recliner, sending shooting pains through her neck. Someone snorts, maybe Dahlia herself. Damn that Muriel and her piercing voice. Dahlia will not speak to her.

"I brought you some fruit juice. Did you finish your sandwich? You don't want the pickle, Dahlia? Think of the starving children in Africa!" Muriel hums, her muscular arms busy as she tidies, moving first the books, then the box of tissues, swirling her cleaning cloth before plonking them back in their places. Her extra chins jiggle with the effort.

Dahlia sips the apple juice, which has been watered down again. Easy on the stomach, the dietician told her. Easy on the budget, Dahlia couldn't resist pointing out in a sour voice. The dietician had frowned and thanked Dahlia for coming to see her.

"Sammy tells me he was by earlier. Isn't he a doll? I just love Sammy to death. Such a charmer, isn't he?" Muriel's cloth continues to swirl, getting closer and closer to the silver picture frame. "You know, he's got children, three of them. Been married ten years. Who'd have thunk it?"

Dahlia is mesmerised by the motion of Muriel's cleaning arm, so much so that she doesn't even see her picking up the photograph.

"You know, Sammy seems to think you had your bath yesterday. Whaddya think of that, Dahlia?"

Dahlia coughs and points at the photograph.

"Put that down, please." Her voice emerges somewhere between a growl and a croak. Muriel gives the glass a quick swirl, and places the frame almost gently back where it belongs.

"That's your late husband, isn't it? My, he's a handsome one. Taken during the War?"

Dahlia nods, but barely.

"Well, I'm pretty sure today's your bath day, but I'll check at the desk." Muriel shakes her head, smiling at the photograph. "I love a man in uniform. My guy's got big eyes, just like that, only blue. What'd you tell me his name was? Ronnie?"

Dahlia closes her eyes, wishing for the burning behind her lids to stop, and for this oversized squawking chicken to go away for good. She slackens her clenched jaw, and hopes Muriel will think she's gone to sleep.

≈

There is a new girl working in the dining room. Dahlia's gaze follows as she moves efficiently around the room, balancing three plates on one arm and carrying a fourth, never dropping a thing. She is tall with cropped hair an unnatural shade of orange. Her unsmiling face holds a youthful fullness, which is betrayed by lean arms poking out from her uniform. White clogs carry her gracefully from table to table.

Dahlia reads the menu card for tomorrow's supper, macaroni or Salisbury steak. The choice she made yesterday for tonight's meal escapes her; as usual, it'll be a surprise. She frowns at the menu, then glances up to see if the girl is any closer to her table. A fine head of orange spikes glows among the crowd of blue and white and bald. She is seated next to that new woman, what is her name? Patterson? No, Nickerson. Last night she dressed for supper in pajamas and high heels, bright red lipstick. Tonight she's dressed properly, but the poor thing can't seem to remember how to eat. The girl is holding her fork loaded with peas, then a piece of white meat. Dahlia holds her breath as Mrs. Nickerson opens her mouth and receives the food like a baby bird, chews slowly, and swallows. Could be chicken, or maybe fish. With a rush of triumph, Dahlia remembers: tonight she will eat fish.

At the next table over, the pigeons, as Dahlia thinks of them, sit hunched in their cardigans, fingers glittering with dinner rings, hair glued into poodle curls, and bright red lipstick slashes against sallow, sagging skin. The pigeons are always burbling about family, daughters this, grandkids that, late husbands and so on. Dahlia prefers to eat alone to keep away the questions, the assumptions.

And how many children have you, Mrs. Miller?

No children, no Missus. Still, *One, a boy,* she'll murmur, when asked. *Lives in Vancouver.* An easy lie so she doesn't have to explain his absence to the busybodies. *No grandkids, although they're trying.* Dahlia is expert at vague non-answers, which roll off her tongue from years of practice, like a politician's smooth response.

Her own private truth is this: There is no son, was never a husband. There was only ever Ronnie.

&

"Would you like the chicken or the fish?"

Ronnie knows she hates chicken, so why bother asking?

"Ma'am?"

It's the new girl, the one with the orange hair. What's that she's got dangling from her ears, fishing lures? And why has she brought two suppers? The girl blinks, slides enormous grey-blue eyes to the left, then back to her.

"Chicken or fish?" She asks.

"Oh. I'll take the fish, please." Dahlia's cheeks burn as the girl leans closer, places the plate before her, and leaves a trail of scent, something like musk, or incense. The earrings dangle prettily, red feathers and beads.

∽

Ronnie only needed to show Dahlia once how to tie a lure. Nimble from years of needlework and knitting socks for the boys overseas, her fingers learned quickly. Ronnie claimed no fish could ever resist one of Dahlia's lures, winking that the lures were as irresistible as Dahlia herself. On their fishing outings, Ronnie always caught the trout, even salmon from time to time, as the two of them trolled the Nova Scotia rivers. Dahlia hated to fish, found the killing and gutting disgusting, but she loved to lie in the boat and doze, watching the clouds overhead and counting the seagulls while Ronnie fished.

Dahlia only ever once caught a fish, and it was purely by accident. Ronnie had left her dozing in the rowboat for a while, lulled by the soft breeze against her skin and the lapping of the water against the wooden hull. When she rolled her head to the side, her cheek resting on the floorboard, the water's sound deepened. She straightened her neck and watched the clouds through her lashes. The water sounded farther away, its rhythm lulling her to sleep. With an ill-fated leap, a salmon landed on her, its cold, hard body slapping her legs as it flipped about in a frenzy. Dahlia sat up and screamed, and in her efforts to back away from the fish she fell overboard, wrenching her shoulder. Later, by the fire, she and Ronnie fed each other morsels of the buttery fried fish.

"Guess that one found you harder to resist than your lures, Dale."

Ronnie always made her feel better.

❧

Dahlia eases herself back into her recliner, pushes the walker away, and reaches for her book. Margaret Laurence's *The Diviners*, for the fourth time. Or is it the fifth? It's the only thing on the book cart that ever interests her. "Spiels on Wheels," Sam calls it. She simply cannot bring herself to read one of those ghastly, well-thumbed romance novels with their silly heroines and plots that have nothing to do with her. That Morag Gunn, with her salty tongue and her hardscrabble life, is more to Dahlia's liking. Not to mention the author. Now, there's someone she can admire.

"Hellooo, Dahlia!" Muriel surges into her room with a shrill twitter, all smiles and double chins. Behind her stands Stella, chocolate arms crossed, her face stern.

"Time for your bath, dear. I checked at the desk, and you're on today."

Dahlia's stomach lurches, and as she tries to stand up and get away from these people, her legs fail her.

"Come on, Dahlia honey, let's get you ready. Stella's here to help."

Dahlia closes her eyes and submits to the indignity of being undressed, her arms shoved into her robe, and then she is propelled to the tub across the hall. Eyes still closed, she pretends to herself that this is all right, that it's perfectly normal for an old woman to have her privates washed by two of the ugliest women God ever created.

Old Woman.

Dahlia thinks of the new girl with the orange hair and

the fishing lures, and wishes a smile on the girl's face. Her eyes are so like Ronnie's, she can't help but think.

༜

When the news came of Ronnie's brother, Dahlia left school for good and packed her belongings, her mind made up. She would take care of her beloved, broken Ronnie, move in and quietly go about running the little house on the edge of town. She would see to it that the scrawny horse had his oats, the chickens their feed. She would gather the eggs and cook them, and clean up Ronnie's neglected mess. In doing so, Dahlia ended her parents' dreams of her marrying the young minister down the road and producing grandchildren for them to dote upon.

Her father had thundered and raged, bellowing that she was no daughter of his, and no longer welcome in the Miller family home. Her mother bore the scene with tearful silence. As Dahlia struggled out the back door with her belongings in a trunk, her mother hugged her and slipped something into her coat pocket. Later, Dahlia removed the photograph of her family from the silver frame, tossed it into the stove, and replaced it with the only picture she could find of Ronnie's brother, taken just before he shipped out.

"Jimmy knew when the picture was taken, he might only live another six months," Ronnie said bitterly. But the photo was allowed to stay in its new frame and in its place of honour, on the table by the bed. His gleaming brown eyes practically jumped out of the frame.

❧

"How ya doing today, Miss Dee? Look, I brought you something. Mind if I sit down?"

Dahlia nods, and Sam perches on the edge of her bed. His face is bright with expectation as he holds a paper bag to his chest. Such a nice young man. What was it Muriel said, something about children?

"Children? Yep, I got three of them. Here, let me show you a picture."

Has she really said that out loud? Dahlia smoothes over the surprise, and feigns interest as she looks at the wallet photo of three little blond kids, young enough and similar enough that it's impossible to tell if they're boys or girls.

"That's Taylor on the left, Kelsey and Fran."

Could be boys' names, but maybe not. Who knows these days? For that matter, who ever knew?

Never mind, Sam is thrilled to show her his treasures, so she takes an extra moment to look at them. They really are kind of sweet.

"I think so, too. 'Specially Taylor, she's Daddy's little darlin'. Loves to cuddle up."

Sam stares at the photograph wearing the indulgent smile Dahlia has observed all her life, but has never herself tried on. Why did Jimmy stop by, anyway, just to show her a picture?

"It's me, Miss Dahlia. Sam. I came by to give you something. Say, who's Jimmy, anyway?"

Dahlia sucks in her breath, steals a glance at the silver-framed photograph nearby. When she looks back at Sam, his eyes are on the photograph. Quickly he looks at the paper bag on his lap.

"Here you go, Miss Dee. There's a craft sale downstairs. I bought you these."

Dahlia's eyes widen as Sam pulls something green and woolen from the paper bag. Is it a hat? No, whatever it is, there are two of them.

"Bedsocks!" Dahlia croaks, delighted.

"You seemed kinda tired of these old ones." Sam's smile is huge and his eyes warm as he crouches to remove the old bedsocks and slip on the new ones. His touch leaves her calves tingling, her thoughts complicated.

Dahlia is exhausted by his kindness. She wants to stroke his downy hair, so soft and foreign. Instead she tucks her hands into her sweater pockets and remembers to thank him.

❧

"I hear you've got a new boyfriend, Dahlia. I'm right jealous, I am!"

Even Muriel's daft talk can't spoil her good mood.

"Stella told me all about it, how someone special brought you a present. Word gets around here, you know!"

Muriel pulls down the bedsheets, folding them back in a crisp triangle. Then she whirls around the tiny room, picking things up and putting them down again, somehow creating order without really looking like she's doing anything.

"What about these, Dahlia?"

Dahlia looks away, pretends she hasn't heard. There was once another pair just like the old bedsocks dangling from Muriel's chubby fingers. Now they are gone.

Muriel's face softens. "How about I just put them away for now?" She opens the closet and pulls out a drawer, folds the bedsocks and rests them on top of what's there. Then she puts Dahlia through her night-time paces, bustling her to the toilet, preparing her toothbrush, washing her face as though she were a child.

Dahlia groans as Muriel helps swing her legs onto the bed, her hips erupting with pain. As Muriel tucks in the sheets and plumps her pillow, Dahlia wonders about Muriel's other life, the one she must have at home. Is she even married?

"Oh my heavens, yes. Haven't I told you all about my George?"

Dahlia winces and chides herself for thinking out loud again.

"He's a good man, although…."

Muriel is staring at the man in the silver frame. Her eyes are bright with tears.

"It's just that…" Muriel sniffles, shakes her head. "Well. He drinks a lot. Too much, actually." Muriel looks at Dahlia, her face uncharacteristically tired, her eyes deadened. "It's just, why can't people simply be who they are, you know?"

Dahlia looks at Jimmy's photograph. Thinks of Ronnie. Veronica, to the rest of the world. Then she places a weathered hand over Muriel's.

Three

She marvels at the lemons. There is an orderliness about them that brings with it the surprise of tears, that too-familiar burn beneath the eyelids she wishes she could control. But they are perfection, sunshine orbs grown in Spain and stacked here in the produce section on a rainy day in Halifax. Of course she must cry.

"You okay, Miss?"

"Oh yes, thanks, I'm fine. Must be my allergies." Muriel gives a watery smile to the young man who is busy with the grapefruits. 'Caebhon', his name tag reads, which makes Muriel wonder. Capon? No, probably one of those Gaelic names whose pronunciation bears no relation to its spelling. Dark stubble pokes through his pale cheeks, occasional hints of manhood, and there is a ring through one of his nostrils, the reddened skin around it crusty. But Caebhon's blue eyes are kind and she'll take all the kindness she can get.

"Aren't the lemons pretty?" She asks brightly. The young man nods and continues with his grapefruit construction.

To atone for her tears Muriel selects the shiniest yellow fruit. Against her chapped fingers it glows with a pebbly translucence. When was the last time she bought a lemon? With great care she places it in a plastic bag and moves on to the meat department, where chicken thighs are on sale again. Maybe she'll try something different from the usual Shake 'n Bake Original, George's favourite, which she's cooked every Monday for as long as they've been married. Rice instead of frozen french fries, and maybe something green. No cookies this trip; Muriel thinks about fruit instead and doubles back to Produce to inspect the grapes. She can't abide the thought of her mother's good china serving bowl being filled once again with grayish canned beans, so she bags a head of broccoli. She'll take her chances on George's wrath and boil it up to go with the lemon chicken. Thirty-three years is a long time to be eating Shake 'n Bake. It's time for something different.

The kindly young man with the nose ring is gone. Muriel has decided he's working part-time to save for university. He's rebellious enough to damage his nose, and who knows, maybe there's a tattoo somewhere, but he's not stupid. If he were, he'd be off in a strange city washing car windshields on street corners to put together enough change for supper or booze. No, Caebhon has a job and responsibilities. He wants to do something with his life. He has left a perfect pyramid of blushing grapefruit.

The prickle of tears sends Muriel scurrying to the checkout.

❧

"Nosey Parker, you're always meddling in other people's business. Anyone with a ring in his nose oughta be locked up. And whaddya call this, a rubber duck?" George pierces a chicken thigh with his fork and hammers it against the plate. He fixes her with a hard stare, the blue of his irises startling against the clusters of red veins blooming around them. Muriel's shoulders tighten, and her ears ring a familiar warning. Already he has rejected the broccoli, scraped it onto the dog dish before Muriel's back was turned.

Didn't her own mother warn her? "That George Boudreau, he's no better'n his pa, Big Billy. Ever wonder why his right hand was shrivelled up? He smashed it through the stained-glass windah at Saint Agnes Church when Father Campbell refused him communion wine. Big Billy had a piece of glass buried under the skin there the rest of his life, a green triangle, right under the knuckle. Them Boudreaus is mean drunks. You'd be a fool to want to marry one of 'em."

There was a time when George's blue eyes had been clear and kind. He'd fix her with a certain stare and a wink that made her knees wobble and her breath catch, and she'd have to find a place to sit down. Before he went on disability he was even funny at times, telling off-colour jokes that made her blush, but at the same time feel a certain thrill at hearing him talk like that.

How things change. It's been some years since she finally admitted to herself that her mother had been right: George is mean when he's been drinking.

Muriel sighs. She should know better than to tell him about her people-watching. She should know better than to tell him anything at all when his words are running together and his breath foul with drink.

And he's wrong about her. She's not nosey. It's her people-watching skills that make her such a good nurse. Stella, for example, the tall, skinny nurse who looks so fierce. It was Muriel's idea to have her convince old Mr. Walters to hand over the butter knife he'd been threatening to kill himself with just because he was so sure someone was trying to poison his tea. Stella had stood before him with her brown hand held out in front of her for fifteen minutes, telling him over and over again in that dusky voice of hers what a nice man he was, and that no-one at Harbourview Centre would ever want to kill him. And then, just like that, Mr Walters had handed over the butter knife. Muriel had known Stella was the one to do it.

Muriel knows, too, when a new resident is scared of Stella. She sees the look in a patient's eyes when she and Stella introduce themselves on their welcome visit, just a glimmer of fear, or a tightening of old fingers around a cane. Muriel knows, as she did last week when Mrs. Nickerson first arrived, pale and nervous and lost, that sometimes she needs to be extra chipper to help reassure a person that she's in safe hands. In no time at all, Muriel had Mrs. Nickerson smiling and talking about her grandchildren as though they were old friends. The dear woman even had a good-night wave for Stella.

Then there's Dahlia, that sour-faced Cape Bretoner she's been trying for months to befriend. She thinks she's found a way to reach Dahlia through the photograph of her late husband, that good-looking fighter pilot who was killed in the war. The way Dahlia looks at the floor every time Muriel mentions how handsome he was in uniform, Muriel just knows theirs can't have been a happy marriage. She wonders if Dahlia had to wear long sleeves in summer, too. Wonders if she loved her Ronnie anyway, the way she loves her George.

George's chair legs bark against the linoleum as he shoves away from the table. The dog heaves itself out of his way, its wary brown eyes gazing hopefully at the abandoned plate of chicken. Muriel sighs as George rips open the bag of Wonder Bread and slathers a wad of butter on a slice. How does he keep so thin, she thinks, as he downs it in a few bites. The dog looks around nervously and slinks out of the kitchen. George wrinkles his nose.

"What's the matter with that damned dog and his christly farts!"

"That's what happens when you feed him your broccoli," Muriel says, trying to sound cheerful. George glares at her and she braces herself. The vein on his forehead is throbbing. If she'd noticed it she would have kept her trap shut.

"I'll be at the Legion eating a *proper* meal." He grabs his cane. The force of his crazy-blue eyes and the fluttering vein causes Muriel to look down at her hands and her shoulders to rise. The silence pounds the air for what seems like an eternity, broken only by the dog's panting in the next room.

"Christ. You crying again?"

Muriel shakes her head, willing the tears away. If only they wouldn't spill. She bites her lip as a distraction, and to her relief her cheeks remain dry. Finally George limps out the back door, slamming it shut. His fury hangs in the air.

Muriel's shoulders settle. She breathes once, and again more fully. In the brittle silence she looks at George's abandoned supper. Then she reaches over and pulls it towards her, pushing away her own plate, empty but for a tidy stack of bones. The chicken thigh exudes the sunny fragrance of Spain. Muriel brings it to her mouth. It's not so rubbery, not if you cut it up small and chew it good.

She knows George doesn't mean to be harsh. Tomorrow morning maybe he'll apologize and call her his special sweetheart.

⁂

Yesterday's rain has washed the air clean. Muriel buttons her jacket and waves to Jessie-next-door, who is pinning sheets on the line.

"How's Frank doing, Jessie?"

"Same as ever," Jessie replies, the clothes pins clenched between her teeth. "Cranky until I've poured some coffee into him."

"My George is just the same," Muriel says, laughing lightly for Jessie, although she rarely sees him awake before leaving for work. The pot of coffee she leaves for him is empty by the time she comes home, and there is usually a stale toast crust or two in the sink, along with his dirty dishes.

"Think they spend too much time at the Legion, Jessie?"

"I think they spend just the right amount of time at the Legion. Can you imagine how we'd be tripping all over them? Damn, there's the phone again. Fifth time this morning."

The wind lifts a pale blue sheet tethered to Jessie's line. Muriel stands with one hand on the car door, transfixed by the swaying sheet as it catches in its folds the wind and the sun. It becomes a pale blur as her eyes fill.

"Jesusmaryandjoseph," she mutters, landing on the car seat with a grunt. Once upon a time she thought her mother was saying "Jesus Maryanne Joseph," like Maryanne was his middle name and Joseph his last name. Now she knows better.

Now she must fetch Mama and take her to the eye doctor, then rush over to work. Yesterday she told Stella she'd be coming in late, and Stella nodded but said nothing. It isn't as though Muriel takes much time away from work, surely Stella knows that. The two of them have been working the longest of any of the Harbourview Centre staff. Muriel can only think of one time Stella was off, two years ago when her daughter graduated from university. When she returned the next morning, there was a new look in Stella's eyes, a kind of satisfaction she'd never seen in her before. Muriel wishes she could be that pleased about something.

She glances at the dashboard clock and steps on the gas pedal. No matter how early she is, Mama will tell her she's late. Of course there's traffic on the bridge, cars snaking down North Street and covering both lanes over the harbour. While she waits for the knot of cars to sort itself out, she counts the tugboats in the distance, the reflex not to look at the black water below automatic. There is a bank of fog beyond McNab's Island, but the sky over Dartmouth is clear, bluer than Jessie's sheets.

The polite tap of a horn brings Muriel's attention back to the bridge, and finally she is moving, catching up to the car ahead, gliding through the toll booth and past the cemetery where her father is buried.

As usual the eyehole to the apartment door is blocked with her mother's clouded gaze. Muriel breathes deeply and lifts the knocker.

❧

Only once this time does Mama say anything about her weight.

"Your feet must be awful sore in those little shoes."

Muriel doesn't need to look down. She knows the straps are too tight, the flesh of her feet exceeds the boundaries of the shoes. She doesn't need her mother to tell her this. Muriel knows well enough.

"I've been after George to poke an extra hole in the straps, Mama. Really, they're fine. I just love the colour, don't you?"

"With my eyes I can't tell what colour they are, but anyone can see they're too small for you. Shame you inherited your father's big bones, with that pretty face of yours."

Father's big bones. Mama has never forgiven her for being round and stocky like her father. Muriel can't help it that she's not built like a bird. No wonder Mama's always complaining about the cold, there's not an ounce of flesh on her. *That pretty face.* Muriel has her mother's facial features, at least the younger, cupid-like version of her mother, with her large brown eyes and bow-shaped mouth. And she makes the most of it, although George disapproves of the collection of Dollar Store lipsticks she keeps in the vanity drawer, Tuscan Orange, Indian

Sunset, Malibu Pink, exotic and mysterious sounding. Muriel has never been farther away than Antigonish. Her lipstick collection allows her at least the thought of travel, not that she'd ever really want to go anywhere special.

"Doctor says he can't do the operation for another two weeks." Her mother's voice, once melodic, is now a flinty rasp. "Seems a long time to wait."

"That's nothing, Mama. Most people have to wait months for cataract surgery."

"Well, it's a wait for someone who likely isn't long for this world."

"Don't be silly, Mama." A childish knot grips her innards every time her mother talks like this. "You're only eighty-two years old. A spring chicken!"

"Never mind 'spring chicken'. I just wish he could do it this week. I'm tired of listening to *Jeopardy*. I'd rather look at Alex Trebek than listen to him."

"You should be excited, Mama. Just think, you'll be able to see properly in two weeks!"

The look her mother gives her could peel paint.

"What's to look at, at my age?"

For all that Muriel tries to point out the good in life, Mama's bad temper always seems to win.

An ugly little thought flits through Muriel's mind. What if the doctor's hand slips, and he slices a hole in Mama's eyeball?

That'd put an end to the remarks about her weight.

❦

Bananas. Oranges. Tomatoes. Iceberg lettuce. Pink grapefruit.

The pen in her hand hovers over the last item on her list. Maybe that nice young man will be at the Superstore again today. What was his name, Calvin? No, it's something she might never pronounce, never remember. Fruits, vegetables, healthy food. Today she will pass by the cookie aisle altogether.

It's not that she's fat. Muriel can't help it that she's inherited her father's big bones, as Mama says. On her brothers the bones worked. The boys all excelled in sports and took jobs in construction, the shipyards. Only now that they're retired are they showing a little paunch, finding it a chore to climb a ladder on the odd cash-only jobs that help pay off their poker debts. But that George! He can eat everything under the sun and still he's nothing more than skin and bones. Wiry and strong he was, as a young man. How she loved watching him scale the roof with a mouthful of nails and his hammer, tacking down the shingles after a storm. He could climb anything, chase a cat up a tree if he wanted to. Her mother always said it was the Mohawk in him, as though pointing out some defect. This exotic part of George's heritage had appealed to Muriel from the beginning. She'd have sworn his eyes, although blue, were almond shaped as his paternal ancestors' were. Mama, on the other hand, was relieved they were blue. No giveaway there.

George's grand-uncles had all worked on the skyscrapers of New York. Fearless and balanced, not a one of them had fallen into the concrete canyon they were helping to build.

There is a photograph of the four of them on their lunch break, three lean young men sitting on a girder, swinging their legs and chewing on sandwiches, grinning at the camera, the fourth smoking a cigarette and looking across the skyscrapers toward the Manhattan Bridge. Titled "Indian Ironworkers," the photograph had been in the National Geographic magazine. George keeps a creased copy of it in a frame hanging on the bedroom wall.

Forty years on, George was by far the best worker on the McKay Bridge. Once he found his place above the water that summer of '68, he was addicted. The bridge became his mistress.

Muriel has never forgotten the metallic taste of fear every morning when George would kick-start his motorbike, tip his hard-hat to her, and with a gleam in his eye speed off as the sun rose over the harbour. Those were happy days for George. For them both. He always gave her a kiss at the end of the day, and he took to calling her his special sweetheart, and every time he did so, Muriel's knees weakened and her face warmed in a blush. But it terrified her to think that three hundred feet above the water he'd clambered and swung, riveting and painting while the black water below waited. He never so much as dropped a screw.

When George's brother Rick went down, still drunk from the previous night's bender, the bridge crew offered to strike a day out of sympathy.

"What do they want to do that for," he'd snorted. "Damned fool'd done up his harness right, he'd be playing cards at the Legion Sar'dy night along with the rest of us. Serves the bastard right."

Rick's funeral was attended by twenty or so of the bridgemen. His wife sat in the front pew, alone but for her brood of scruffy boys in a restless row beside her. The youngest cried for his papa, and the older three took turns at hitting one another, furtive, quick slaps which their dazed mother seemed not to notice.

It was late that night and blistering cold when George had staggered through the kitchen door in a drunken fury. Muriel lay in the dark, the blanket pulled up over her head, as George lurched around in the kitchen, his bellowing a harsh counterpoint to the sound of scraping chair legs, slamming cupboard doors and shattering glass. When finally he made his way upstairs, groaning as he pulled himself up by the banister, Muriel reached for the metal flashlight. It was cold in her shaking hand, a slight reassurance to know she might use it to defend herself if necessary.

George kicked at the bedroom door. His second kick rattled Muriel's perfume bottles on the dresser. His final kick sent the door slamming against the wall with such force, the National Geographic photograph of his grand-uncles tumbled to the floor. The flashlight shook in Muriel's hand as she raised it above her head, ready. But all she needed it for was to illuminate her weeping husband who was on the floor doubled in pain, three of his toes splayed and his ankle swelled to the size of a baseball, wailing for his lost brother.

When the grey light of dawn crept between the slats of the blind, she bound his foot and slept.

And that was the end of his affair with the bridge. He has not walked properly since.

❧

Pink grapefruit. Muriel lifts the pen, which has left an ink blob where the *t* is crossed. She takes the shopping bag from its hook by the door, fishes for her keys in her purse. Freshens her lipstick, Malibu Pink. Opens the door and steps outside and breathes in the smell of thawing leaves.

Her first stop is the produce section. Apples the colour of celery. Pomegranates – they mystify her – where in the world do they grow them, and how do you eat them? Cantaloupe. How to tell if they're ripe? Once she cut one open only to find it hard and unappetizing, its shiny orange flesh a lie. She lifts one and stares at its green-brown skin, pitted like the back of a toad. Brings it to her ear and shakes it, hoping to hear the secret of its ripeness. She stares at it again, and moves to put it down.

"Give it a sniff."

Muriel starts, and turns to see Caebhon, as his name tag reminds her, with his dark curls, wide-set eyes the colour of ice, and the ringed nostril.

"If it smells like cantaloupe, then it'll taste like cantaloupe. Kind of like strawberries do. Smell like they taste, that is." His smile is lazy and sweet. Muriel closes her gaping mouth with a snap, and brings the melon to her face.

"Smells like cantaloupe to me," she twitters.

"*Kevin to Customer Service, please? Kevin to Customer Service?*"

Caebhon's eyes travel up towards the crackling voice in the loudspeaker, and he looks toward the Customer Service counter.

"Nice fresh lemons today," Kevin-spelled-Caebhon says with a wink, and turns and hurries away as Muriel smiles, places the melon in her cart, and waits for tears that do not come.

Four

How Violet wishes, sometimes, that she were deaf like so many of the others. All around her, old people chatter and drone, their voices elevated beyond what is tolerable in the real world, their responses automatic and utterly predictable. Politely not listening to a word being said to them.

Yes, yes. Oh my, you don't say. For heaven's sake.

At the next table, old ladies in drab cardigans and gaudy lipstick compare dull notes on children, grandchildren, tonight's supper of boiled chicken and peas. Violet sighs and reaches for the pepper. Nothing here is beautiful, not even the food.

For a moment she thinks of tomorrow's bath. She closes her eyes and imagines the warmth, the fragrance of bath oil, the tingling of her scalp as strong fingers massage shampoo into what remains of her hair. Violet's life has been reduced to so few pleasures; her weekly bath has become a regular high point. Perhaps Estella will help.

Most of the frail old birds around here are frightened of Estella, stuck on ancient fears instilled by their parents who might have been alive long enough ago to remember the daughters and sons of black Loyalists who probably cleaned their houses, drove their carts, and worse. Certainly they remember the shacks clustered along the windy shore of the Bedford Basin, the warnings to stay away at all cost, their own blind eyes turned when the shantytown was razed and the dark-skinned residents made to live elsewhere. How long ago was that? Thirty years? Fifty? Some days the past is a knot of confusion, events overlapping that should be spaced years apart. Except for Violet's early days, her days of sun and beauty.

There is a new resident sitting alone at a far table, a Mrs. Nickerson. She is daffy and prim, Violet has decided. Last night she came to dinner dressed in her nightie and high heels, shiny black pumps more suited to an evening at the opera than to baked beans and toast in the dining hall. She carried a matching black evening bag.

Violet watched, fascinated, while the woman ate. She opened her mouth in a small o to let past the three or four beans perched on her fork, masticated for a full minute before swallowing, and then she wiped her mouth with her napkin, around and around so as not to miss a speck of lipstick. After sitting still a moment, she opened her evening bag and pulled out a shiny, gold lipstick tube. Looking straight ahead, she replenished the colour on her thin, white lips, then she picked up her fork and allowed a few more beans past her freshened mouth, chewed for a minute, swallowed, and performed the whole exercise all over again until the plate of beans was empty and the skin around her mouth red with being rubbed. Mrs. Nickerson pushed the plate away and stood, and with her back straight as a rod she walked with great purpose across the dining hall, never once wobbling on her high heels.

Tonight Mrs. Nickerson is dressed in a matching pantsuit, blue, with a yellow scarf at her throat. On her feet are fluffy white slippers. When the girl with the orange hair sets down the plate of boiled chicken before her, Mrs. Nickerson looks bewildered. The girl frowns, then sits in the empty chair beside her, spears a few peas and holds the fork in front of her. There is a tattoo on her skinny forearm, but at this distance Violet cannot make it out. Finally, Mrs. Nickerson opens her mouth and takes the peas. Then with a slow hand she takes the fork and stares for a moment before recognizing with a delighted smile that this is her supper. She eats, and eats some more. The girl with the tattoo watches a moment, then gets up and continues with her work while Mrs. Nickerson devours her supper. There is no sign of the evening bag, and her lips are bare.

҂

Violet places her purse in the desk drawer, locks it, and shivers as the key slips back down between her breasts on its string. It's nearly time for *Jeopardy* and the nightly ritual of walkers and canes abandoned along the wall of the lounge while their owners sit staring at the TV, biding their while until bed. *What is quince? Who is Winston Churchill?*

There is mail, a pink envelope, greeting-card shaped. It sits propped against the telephone, addressed to Auntie Vi Crenshaw. Melanie, her niece, has finally written. It's about time.

Violet eases herself into her chair and reaches for the letter-opener, first blowing the dust off of it before inserting it into the corner of the envelope. She must speak to someone about the dust in here, perhaps that nice Sam. He seems to be the only one who gets things done.

A Hallmark card with violets on the cover. Violet sighs and shakes her head, imagining her niece's delight at finding such a card to send to her.

Dear Auntie Vi:

First of all, I must ask how you are keeping in your new residence. Is the food all right? Have you made some new friends? How is the nursing care? I was so sorry to hear about your broken wrist. I hope it's healing nicely.

And now I must thank you for the painting, which arrived just after Christmas. Even though the model is naked I have it hanging in the TV room – it goes perfectly with the couch – and every time I look at it I'm thrilled. I wish I could visit and have you tell me the story behind it. The young woman is so beautiful! You can't quite see her face from behind the piece of silk she's holding, but somehow she radiates such joy. I just love the golden light – the painter was obviously quite talented. I've seen paintings in the National Gallery that aren't half as good.

Maybe next summer we can have our visit. If Mike can get away from work we plan to make a run to the outlet stores in the States. We could stop in Halifax on our way there.

Anyway, I just wanted to let you know how much I appreciate your sending me the painting. You've left it in good hands.
    Fondly,
    Melanie

A wry smile spreads across Violet's cheeks. Her wrist is fine, thank you, just a bit achy on cold days. After a few months of physiotherapy it's a little bent, but still strong enough to hold a pencil and to brush her teeth. How nice that the painting "goes" with Melanie's sofa. At least the girl sees the light, the movement, the emotion of the painting. She seems to appreciate the painter's skill, that much she has taken in over the years Violet has spoken to her of great works of art, shown her what she could. And this one, "Golden Nude," is truly one of the greatest watercolours Violet has ever seen.

The placement of the silk, suspended over the subject's face, denies Melanie the one small hint as to who the model was. Those many years ago, the artist placed the silk deliberately, in favour of realizing the flaw he could not bear, the asymmetry of the model's face. Asymmetry had been repugnant to him, produced a physical reaction in him similar to food poisoning. It was no wonder that the model's brown eye, paired with the blue one, turned his stomach. No wonder he had to cover it.

But what mystery and joy that one gesture gives the painting! Sunlight pours through the silk from behind, and there is no knowing where the silk ends and the model's hair begins, a cloud of golden light. Her face is irrelevant; the joy radiates from the light she holds aloft.

Perhaps she will tell the story of the nude to Melanie. Violet has given the girl the painting, so she might as well give her the story behind it as well. Summer is a long time from now; who knows if she will be around to tell her? And how much she will tell? There is a lined notebook in the desk drawer, empty but for a Christmas card list she had to abandon when her wrist was broken. Later today she will begin, but for now Violet closes her eyes, leans her head against the wing of her chair and invites sleep to come.

Snow dusts the far mountains, and the sky is of a blue that brings her tears. How desperately the parched land needs rain. There is a dry wind, unpleasant in its restlessness. It seems to come from everywhere; there is no escaping it blowing around her legs and forcing the skirt above her knees. Nearby a flock of wild parrots dips and soars among the kapok trees, making an unseemly racket as they try to outwit the wind. Violet must hurry and get to the studio, she mustn't be late.

ॐ

The Christmas card list is shorter than she'd remembered, much diminished as one by one her friends and acquaintances have died off. Melanie's name is at the top of the list, Violet's only family member taking precedence over the rest, now that her friends are mostly gone. Is it too late to send Christmas greetings now? Violet looks out the window at the leaden March sky, the choppy, cold water. Not a sailboat on the harbour on a raw day like this. Violet draws her shawl tightly around her, for no matter how high the artificial heat in this place, she is always cold. How she misses the desert heat. She turns the page and begins to write:

Dear Melanie,

I am so glad you like the painting. It really is quite special. You may recall it hanging in my apartment over the bed for all those years. Just as it pleases me to have given it to you, it would please me to tell you what I know of it, how it came to exist. I hope you will find it interesting.

Violet lays down the pencil, stretches her fingers before a kink sets in. She still does not know exactly what she will tell her niece. With a sigh she picks up the pencil; she might as well start somewhere as nowhere.

At the far end of the studio before the window, there was an old wooden chair draped in muslin yellowed with age and the sun. The artist peered around the canvas and nodded. Not a word from him, only the slightest glance. I loosened the sash on my robe and sat.

There is a discreet tap at the door.

"Time for your bath, Miss Crenshaw."

Violet closes her notebook and turns to see Estella standing tall in the doorway.

"Come in, Estella. I'm nearly ready."

Relieved, Violet allows her to help with the buttons of her blouse, ease her arms into the bath robe. She likes Estella's quiet manner, and there is a directness to her wide-eyed stare that appeals to her own, frank nature. Besides, with her high cheekbones and cat-like eyes, along with the full lips, Estella is a rare thing around here, a great beauty, even if she is beyond her prime. Violet's fingers twitch for her pencil, and she casts a look at her notebook. The impulse startles her; it's been a long time since she ventured to draw.

"You've been writing, Miss Crenshaw."

It is a statement, not a question.

"Yes, yes I have."

"A writer, huh."

Again, a statement. Estella helps her out of her bathrobe.

"Not really. Although I've always wanted to be."

"Never too late to start."

Estella holds Violet by the waist and lowers her into the fragrant froth. Violet sighs as the warm water surrounds her. She dreads the coming shock of cold air against her skin, but will enjoy every minute of her bath. Estella sits back and gives her some extra moments of near-privacy before bathing her. Violet rests her head against a folded towel, closes her eyes, and thinks about what she will write for Melanie. There is so much in the telling and the not-telling; she must organize her thoughts.

&

Indeed, I was scared. What young woman wouldn't be, posing nude for the first time? But I had attended life drawing classes, had learned to appreciate the shapes and form, shadows and light that constitute a human being and translate to composition. When our instructor's model took sick with the galloping consumption, he posted the announcement:

"Any female art student wishing to pose for me will be granted instruction free of cost for the duration of the next session. Reply by calling card."

I was starved to learn more, and prepared to do almost anything to learn it. So there I sat, frightened, on a hard chair in an older man's studio, in the name of art. His art, and I hoped, mine.

෨

When she is dried off and dressed, her skin silken against her cotton nightie, Violet looks again at Estella's face. There is hardly a line, even though the woman must be near fifty, or who knows, even sixty. It is impossible to tell.

"May I draw you sometime?" Estella blinks and looks away. Violet has never seen Estella caught off-guard, embarrassed. "Only if you'd like me to, that is," she adds. "You have an interesting face. Lots of planes and shadows."

Estella glances out the window for a moment, then nods slightly.

"Yeah, sure. Sometime when I'm not too busy."

Violet hopes she means it, that she's not just saying it to be polite.

"Thank you, Estella. And for the bath."

Estella nods and almost smiles, Violet can tell by the slight rise in her cheekbones. She returns to her desk and opens her notebook, picks up the pencil and continues scribbling:

"Not yet," he croaked. I held the robe against my chest while he disappeared once again behind the easel. For some moments he tamped at the paint on his palette. The smell of oil and turpentine was making me queasy, so I busied myself with counting the brushes drying in a cup nearby. How I longed to grasp a brush, to stain a canvas with colours of my own making.

Finally, "Now," came his gruff command.

It was my mother's robe, of Japanese silk, brought back to her from the Orient by a beau when she was a young woman. Green it was, slashed with embroidered black stalks of grass and birds in flight. I did not wish to drop it on the filthy floor, so I tiptoed to another chair where I draped it. The breeze from the window caught and moved it, animating the birds.

৵

Violet's earliest memory is of birds in flight, or so it seemed at the time. She can't yet have been out of diapers.

The air was moving with smoke and music. The floor shook with stamping, kicking feet, and laughter rang out from the row of dancing birds. From atop their perfect heads arose fountains of colour, green, yellow, blue and orange, although Violet had no words yet for feathers. Or colours, for that matter. One by one the birds flew toward her, smiling, laughing, swooping their wings as she regarded them from her perch in the push-chair, kicking her feet in delight, causing the wheels beneath her to squeak in time. There was a sudden shout, a man's voice which stilled the air and quieted the birds whose smiles vanished. They all looked toward the voice. The blue one, her mama, then looked to the ground.

Violet remembers being drenched in sorrow over the silencing of her birds. Even now, just thinking of it, she is surprised by the depth of her emotion. Now that she is old and alone, everything she feels is amplified: minor irritations, confusion, and the odd moments of joy. Mostly remembered, it all exhausts her. But it is sadness that is the most difficult to bear.

She knows now that the man's voice was her father's, the birds, dancers, and that the blue bird, her mama, had been singled out and humiliated by Papa. This is her only memory of her father, who, soon after the incident with the birds, simply was gone. All she has of him is the sound of his shout, which has surely been coated over the years by the dust of imagination and memory.

There was never a sense of loss over him on her mother's part, a notion that anything was missing. As she thinks about it, it strikes Violet that her mother was probably more complete without him, certainly freer to live her bohemian life. To young Violet, her blue-feathered mother had given her a first glimpse of delicate beauty, and that is far more important than the paternal spectre that has lingered and occasionally enticed her.

❧

Mrs. Nickerson is standing at the doorway, looking around the dining hall. Her mouth is pursed, her eyebrows furrowed, and even as Mr. Walters struggles to get around her with his walker, she does not move. Mrs. Nickerson is lost,

Violet realizes with a sympathetic jolt. Violet looks around for the girl, the one with the tattoo on her arm, but she is nowhere in sight. She puts her hand on her cane and is about to ease herself out of the chair and do what? Help the woman? But there is no need; at next glance Mrs. Nickerson is being led to her table, her face tentative as Estella guides her by the arm, talking quietly while she helps her to her chair. Mrs. Nickerson will not look her saviour in the eye, but gives a frightened nod as Estella turns to leave.

There is always work to be done by the nurses, and Violet has never seen any of them standing still. Estella walks out of the cafeteria tall and sure, moving with grace. She could have been a dancer at one time, thinks Violet.

&

She flips to the back page of her notebook. The blank sheet of paper, scored with faint blue lines and the pink margin, waits. Who ever decided on blue lines and pink margins, Violet wonders. And why has she turned away from her writing? Her pencil settles halfway down the page, and she moves her hand in a triangular gesture. Then another triangle, followed by two slashes. Some cross-hatch and a few more lines, quick and precise. Estella.

Violet feels the echo of Estella's bath-time touch; tries to remember the last time anyone has touched her voluntarily, intimately. It's been so long she can't possibly choose a memory from a particular year, even a decade in her life. Twenty years, perhaps thirty. She looks once more at Estella's likeness, the cat-like eyes situated over the checkbones, triangles upon triangles. It's been years since she has drawn anyone. There hasn't been anyone worth drawing. Slowly she turns the pages back to the beginning of the notebook and reads the first few lines.

"What's that you're writing, Miss Crenshaw?"

Violet catches her breath and turns to see Sam at the door, bearing her morning snack. A nice young man, if rather bland looking.

"Oh, it's just...." His interested brown eyes make up for the potato shape of his face. "I'm writing some things down for my niece," Violet says.

"I didn't know you had a niece. Does she live in Halifax?"

"No, no, she lives in Ottawa. But she's coming to visit, maybe in July."

"That'll be nice for you. Have I seen her around here before?"

"No, not yet. She's very busy with her work. She's a systems analyst, you know."

"Something to do with computers, eh?"

Sam shrugs and grins. Clearly he knows little more about that sort of thing than Violet does. His smile is infectious, welcoming. It's nice to talk to someone.

"She's my only family, you know. My sister died when Melanie was a little girl. She was very young when it happened. It was terribly sad."

Has she really given that much away to this nice man with the kind face?

"Did you raise her, then?"

"Partly, Sam. Partly." Violet thinks of the cheques she has written over the years to pay for the girl's schooling, to help her dimwitted father buy her suitable clothes and send her to summer camp. How she would have loved to take the girl in, have her close and raise her, someone to call her own.

"You'll be happy to see her, then."

"Hmm? Oh, this summer, yes. Yes, I will."

"Not everyone is, you know." Sam gives her a wink. "Happy to see family, that is."

"Yes, I suppose I've reached the age where I should be able to choose who I'd like to spend time with. You, for instance."

Sam laughs quietly and sets her snack on the table by her chair.

"Let's talk again soon, Sam."

"Any time, Miss Crenshaw. Happy writing."

Violet feels a long-ago warmth in her belly, thanks to this generous man with the interesting face.

❧

Tonight's fish, white and wet, sits untouched on Violet's plate. She has picked at the peas and managed a few mouthfuls of dry rice, but the fish is in desperate need of some lemon. Here they are living by the sea, and no-one around here knows how to serve fish. Violet will flag down the orange-haired girl once she has finished serving. Surely there must be a lemon rolling around in the kitchen, somewhere.

Mrs. Nickerson's chair is empty. It's been two lunches now and two suppers since Violet has seen her. She wonders if any of the ladies at the next table have noticed. She waves at the girl, who nods, raises her finger to wait a minute, and disappears through the swinging door to the kitchen.

Is Mrs. Nickerson ill? Violet wonders. Has her family taken her home for a few days? Maybe she's in hospital. Things come on quickly for the old ones. For all of them, if they wait around long enough.

"Can I get you something, Mrs. Crenshaw?"

"That's *Miss* Crenshaw." Immediately Violet wishes she could take back the haggish-sounding reproach. She winces, tries to smile. "Is there any lemon? I'd be glad of a slice of lemon with my fish."

"Sure thing, Miss Crenshaw. Be right back."

Violet stares at Mrs. Nickerson's empty chair. She is not sure why the preoccupation, why she can't keep her eyes off it.

"Here you go, Miss Crenshaw."

"Thank you very much. Say, before you go…"

"Is there anything else you'd like?"

The girl is waiting. Perhaps Violet should speak.

"Can you tell me why Mrs. Nickerson's chair is empty? You know, the new lady who sits over there by herself."

The girl's eyes flit in the direction of the empty chair, and then towards the floor before returning to Violet's.

"Mrs. Nickerson passed on yesterday morning."

Violet breathes in sharply. The daffy, prim lady has died suddenly.

"But she's new, she…she's only been here a week," Violet stammers.

"Was she a friend of yours, Mrs. Crenshaw?"

Violet does not bother to correct the girl.

"No. Not a friend." Not a friend, but a comrade, she thinks to herself. She gathers her wits, and tries on a pleasant smile for the girl. Hopes the tickle on her cheek is not a tear making its way down among the creases. "Thank you for the lemon slice," she says.

"You're welcome. Any time."

The hand that belongs to the tattooed arm rests on Violet's wrist. It is a Celtic knot, Violet can see now, one of those eternal love designs in the bruised-blue typical of tattoos. Although it is small, there is barely room for it on the skinny arm. The girl gives her hand a squeeze, and dashes off to the kitchen.

ॐ

Violet lays down the pencil and rubs her wrist. She has written nonstop for the last hour, forgoing *Jeopardy* in favour of finishing her story for Melanie. The ache is deep, her fingers tired and stiff. Foolish to think she could get it all down in one sitting; even if she'd never broken it, it is an eighty-three-year-old wrist.

"Time to get ready for bed, Miss Crenshaw."

Estella's deep voice is like a balm.

"I'm afraid I can't hold the toothbrush tonight, Estella." A rush of shame warms Violet's face.

"Your wrist bothering you again?"

"Yes, I've overdone it with my writing."

"Here, I'll rub some of this on it."

She pulls up the desk chair close, takes Violet's hand in hers and rubs in the salve. Estella's fingers are impossibly long, her dusky skin smooth and unmarked by age. With swift motions she rubs more and more deeply into her wrist, releasing the ache.

"Shame about Mrs. Nickerson," Violet says, feeling the need for words to fill the silence.

Estella's eyes grow distant. "It was quick and merciful," she says in a low voice.

"Did she have family?"

"Yes, a son and his wife. Two grandsons."

The family must be scrambling to arrange the visitation, the funeral service, thank-you notes to all who have condoled. Violet tries to imagine the two grandchildren comforting one another. She hopes their parents will tell them fond stories and make a legend of their grandmother.

"You must be writing a book." Estella's strong fingers continue to slide around her wrist, her forearm.

"It's a story, of sorts. For my niece. I gave her a painting, and now I want to tell her a little bit about it."

"A little bit," Estella nearly laughs.

"Well, it's a long story."

"She'll be glad of it."

"I hope so."

"I hope it's worth the sore wrist." Estella gives her a final rub. "Think you can hold a toothbrush now?"

Violet rotates her hand. Not perfect, but at least it won't keep her awake tonight. "Yes, I think so. It feels much better. Thank you, Estella."

While Estella disappears into the bathroom to get her toothbrush, Violet opens her notebook to the last page. Perhaps Estella won't like it, will not see herself in the doodle.

Suddenly she is there, holding the toothbrush and a glass of water.

"Look, I…" Violet begins, but Estella is already looking at the drawing, her eyes opened wide.

"That's me, isn't it?"

"Yes, yes it is. Do you like it?"

There is a silence which Violet fills with doubts.

"No-one's ever drawn me before," Estella says. "It really looks like me."

"You've been awfully busy, so I did it from memory. I'd like you to have it."

A shy smile crosses Estella's generous mouth. It is the first time Violet has ever seen her smile.

᷒

From behind the easel there was a cough.

"Sorry, sir, it's just that my robe fell on the floor, and…." But why bother to explain? I resumed my position on the chair.

"Arms," came his voice. I hesitated, wondering exactly what it was he wanted me to do with them.

"Up, please. Over your head."

I complied, enjoying the sun's warmth on my back while he painted.

"Hold this, please, like that," he said, placing a strip of silk in my hands and gesturing. I held it up and slightly over my head, my

arms spread wide. He fiddled with it until it was hanging before my face, then returned to his stool. There was more tamping of paint on the palette, followed by a frustrated noise.

"Excuse me. Your... they need to be more... more... pronounced."

The heat of the day had relaxed my skin, altering its texture. With his gaze averted from my face he reached for me with a dry brush, gazing with intent and sitting as far from me as his reach would allow. The arcs beneath his fingernails were permanently stained with paint, splashes of my own skin tones mingling with the skin of his fingers, overlapping with the stick of the brush. Quickly he worked the brush in small circles until my flesh complied. I'm certain I blushed, and to distract myself I watched the sinews of his arms working beneath fine, golden hairs.

"Yes, like that," he muttered and retreated behind the easel.

Turning my head so I could see beyond the silk, I gazed out the window at the San Gabriel Mountains while the shadows of rare clouds made their way across the horizon, chasing the sun. What kept my aching arms in the air was the hope that once the painting was completed, he would show me how to capture the light dancing on the mountains so I might put it to a canvas of my own.

Soon the sun would leave my back, withdraw from the tangles of my hair. Perhaps there would finally be rain.

෨

Her story is not exactly dining hall chat, anything that would interest the cardigan ladies. It might shock them to an early grave. Well, earlier, anyhow. Somehow Violet doesn't think any of it would warrant the usual, *Oh my, you don't say. For heaven's sake.*

She is grateful, in a way, to Mrs. Nickerson. Her sudden passing was what Violet needed to finish the story for her niece. Perhaps Melanie will keep the notebook somewhere safe, and years from now when they are old enough, show it to her children. "That beautiful lady with the sun in her hair was my Auntie Vi, your great-aunt. There is silk over her face because her eyes were just like yours, just like mine, one brown and one blue. She was the artist's muse."

Violet pulls the blanket around her shoulders, warm for the first time since her weekly bath. In darkness beneath the covers she rubs the tingling skin above the ache, trying to recreate Estella's touch. Violet will never again see the painting, she is certain.

Five

She whispers her mother's words, written in a fine, but practical hand, private musings on the garden she built so long ago. The remembered sound of Mother's voice, wrapped in the scent of earth and blossoms and a warm summer breeze, brings Myrna comfort, transports her from this cold and foreign place.

April 29ᵗʰ, 1932

There is no bulb that shows such savage energy in breaking through the earth as the Emperor daffodil; there is a crack a foot long in the earth with a mound in the centre; lift a bit of earth off that mound and there are the stout green spikes of life and hope. There is a lusty exuberance to the growth of the Emperors which is a great delight to me.

How she misses the force of her mother's love, her particular brand of "lusty exuberance." Myrna runs a finger down the page, as though by touching the ink she might bring her back, even after all these years. She closes the diary and straightens the cuffs of her cardigan.

Myrna laments her own lack of exuberance. How long has it been since she was thrilled by anything? She has become what she once scorned, a dull old lady in a nursing home. Lipstick might help brighten things. There must be a tube in her purse; before lunch she will root around for it.

Stuck to the back cover of the diary there is a torn newspaper clipping, the yellowed and fragile remains of her father's obituary. His bespectacled face with its tidy moustache peers out from the clipping. *Mourning the Passing of J. W. Shaw*, the headline reads. Myrna skims over the words, memorized from a thousand readings. When first she discovered the diary she tried to ease the clipping away from the back cover, but it held on like skin, stuck fast from decades spent in storage in her mother's airless attic. Better to leave it be; at least she still has it. Myrna opens the drawer to her writing desk and places the journal where it will await her next reading.

Myrna could use a cup of tea. She looks at the walls, painted a cold white that wouldn't be her choosing. Mother would have insisted on pale green, the better to show off her artwork. But there is no artwork, not here. Not since Myrna handed over the old Portland Street house key to her son and came here with two suitcases. Instead of art there are six framed photographs hanging in a row, reaching into Myrna's past. In four of them her grandchildren force stiff smiles, some with the gleam of hardware on their teeth. Years out of date, but their childhood is the era by which she knows them best. Peter, her son, and his wife Elizabeth peer out of another, posed with their heads at odd angles and with their university diplomas clutched in young hands; and the last, taken sixty-three years ago, is her wedding photograph. How simple her dress was, ivory silk, and how handsome Frank looked in his naval uniform. Mother was besotted with Frank. "I love a man in uniform," she would say, winking at her own husband, J.W., who never failed to blush when she spoke like this.

Tea with Mother – where would they both sit in this small room? At the Portland Street house they would have sat comfortably in the parlour, on the velvet upholstered chairs and surrounded by floral wallpaper, polished wood, and Mother's art collection: the "Blue Boy" reproduction peering at them from within an ornate frame, and the silhouettes of Mother and her sisters, relics of their West Indian childhood; Father's enormous framed map of Halifax from 1853, which has hung over the sofa since before Myrna's birth eighty-four years ago. Perhaps she would light a log in the fireplace to take the nip off the air.

It is cramped in this place, but Myrna could offer the wingback chair to her mother. Perhaps the nurse might move the writing desk to the corner so Myrna can perch on her walker seat. She'll serve cucumber sandwiches and sponge cake with blueberry sauce, Mother's favourite. Tea in the silver service; perhaps Peter can have his wife give it a polish before bringing it over. Yes, she must ask him about that, and then arrange a taxi cab for Mother. Try to find a box of chocolate mints for afters, mother's crystal stem vase and a daffodil from the garden.

They will laugh and talk and Mother will tell stories of her early life in the tropics, of how as a young girl about to depart for England she hid the four silhouettes in the bottom of her steamer trunk, wrapped in her bloomers. Of her romance with J.W. that brought her to Nova Scotia. They will remind each other of this time and that, and Mother's hands will dance in the telling, her amethyst ring throwing sparks about the room.

The knock at the door brings Myrna back to the present, like a slap.

"Lunchtime, Mrs. Willoughby." Nurse Muriel peers around the door, her cheerful face plumped up in a smile. "Shepherd's pie today, dear. How about I start up your walker for you?"

Myrna bites her lip, swallows back the lump in her throat. How silly of her to talk herself into tea with Mother. It's been more than thirty years since last she saw her.

"Just a moment," she mutters, as she opens her purse and commences a slow fumble for her lipstick.

❧

"Is there anything I can bring you from the grocery store, Mum?"

Myrna winces as Elizabeth's hearty voice booms over the telephone line. It's not the loudness that bothers Myrna so much as her familiarity. After all these years, she is still not comfortable with someone else's daughter calling her "Mum."

"Elizabeth means well, my dear," her husband used to say, his blue eyes creased in amusement. "Better she calls you that than 'Hey-you'." Frank always said what she needed to hear.

"No thank you, Elizabeth. I have everything I need."

"You sure, now? Well, how 'bout I stop by for a little visit, anyways. Be around three o'clock, after Oprah."

"That would be nice."

Even her words come slowly now, like everything else.

Mornings, in particular, are slow. The newspaper takes a long time to read, if she even manages to get through it without her arm tiring from holding the magnifier over the page. More often than not, Myrna puts the paper aside and turns on the television. Today is no different, and like every other day, there is nothing interesting to look at. In a way, she looks forward to her visit from Elizabeth. Perhaps she will look at the Oprah show so she might understand what Elizabeth is talking about.

Myrna remembers Frank's excitement when he brought home their first television set. The glass tube was encased in walnut, and it gave off a frightful blue glare that sometimes caused her a headache. But she soon grew accustomed to it, and their evenings became cozy and predictable as they followed the domestic silliness of Lucille Ball and Jackie Gleason. Of course there was also bad news, of that poor young President shot down in cold blood on a November day; and then there was the excitement of the moonwalk, so surreal her mother could not be convinced it wasn't made using actors in a movie studio.

In the end she doesn't make it past the opening credits. Bored by the commercials, Myrna sleeps through Oprah.

❧

"Mother? Mother, it's me, Peter."

Myrna blinks. Blindly she pats her cardigan, finds the string around her neck and works her way down to the glasses, which she slides onto her nose. Peter is sitting perched on her bed.

"Peter, dear, what a lovely surprise," Myrna croaks, then clears her throat. "But where is Elizabeth? I thought she was coming today."

Peter reaches across and switches off the television. He looks pale, and the shadows around his eyes have deepened. He has her brown eyes, his father's hawk nose. His hank of blond hair is receding, but still it falls forward, as it did when he was a boy. Myrna marvels that he is fifty, that she has a son well into his middle age.

"Lizzie's parking the car. She'll be right in."

"Well, I'm so glad you're here. I've been meaning to ask if the Emperor daffodils are up yet. You know, the tall ones by the fence."

"Ah, not sure, Mother. I'll have a look when I go home." Peter runs his hand through his hair, pushing it off his forehead.

"You know, your grandmother first planted them in 1932, just after she and J.W. bought the house. I'm quite sure what's there must be descended from them."

"You don't say."

"My soul, you're a fidget today, aren't you? Look at your feet, tapping away like Fred Astaire!"

"Sorry, Mother. Listen...."

"What is it, dear?" There is something wrong, Myrna knows it from the way Peter is not looking at her. "Is everything all right, Peter?"

The door opens suddenly, and there is Elizabeth, in a whirl. Her hair is pulled back in a tight ponytail, making her face look more pinched than usual. She rushes over to Myrna and pecks her cheek, leaving a minty whiff. Gum, as always; Elizabeth has the most pronounced jaw muscles Myrna has ever seen.

"Hello, Mum! Did Peter tell you our great news?"

"News?"

"Ah, we were just getting to that, Lizzie." Peter's hand is on Elizabeth's arm, guiding her to sit by him on the bed. Myrna feels her stomach tighten.

"What news?" She asks.

"It's actually kind of exciting, Mother. Lizzie and I have, ah, decided to move across the Harbour."

"Move?" Her own voice has the cadence of a petulant child.

"Well, ah, we've found a condo on the Halifax side that we both really like, and..."

"You're gonna love it, Mum, it's right downtown on the waterfront!" Elizabeth is beaming, her teeth whiter than is possible in the natural world.

"Yes, we'll be even closer to you, Mother, a five-minute drive. No more bridge traffic."

Dread washes over Myrna like rain.

"But what about Portland Street, what about Mother's house?"

"It's all taken care of, Mother. We've got the best real estate agent in the city working on it. Matter of fact we've, ah, we've already had an offer. That's sort of what got things moving so quickly."

"Yeah, and wait'll you see what the decorator wants to do with the new place! All modern furniture, leather couches and such. They'll be a breeze to keep clean, a lot easier than velvet."

"Lizzie, please." Peter quiets his wife. "Mother, we need to downsize. The girls are gone, none of them living in Dartmouth. With heating costs being what they are, we can't keep the place up. That massive garden...."

Her son's eyes are wide, fearful. She must try to make this less difficult for him.

"Of course, dear. It is a lot of work." Myrna has regained control of her voice. But oh, her beautiful garden. Mother's daffodils. She arranges a smile for her son.

Peter's face loosens in relief, and his feet stop tapping. Beside him, his wife looks at her watch.

"Are... are you all right about this, Mother?"

"Yes, dear, I understand. You two need a smaller place. It makes perfect sense."

But she doesn't understand. It makes no sense to her at all. She is not ready for this.

Peter kisses her on the cheek, then turns and leaves just in time for her eyes to water, then spill over. Her mother's house, her own home, the garden, sold to a stranger.

∿

February 28th, 1933

Whenever the modest and earthy smell of daffodils comes to my nostrils it brings but one picture to my mind. It is an overgrown and earnest gawk of eleven years sitting at breakfast in a London hotel, surreptitiously sniffing at a vase of narcissi on the table while sunlight streams in through the lace-covered corridors and she painfully struggles to digest new sights, new sounds, new sensations – not the least of the latter being a new and scratchy serge dress and heavy laced boots on the feet which had been free for eleven years. In a way the smell of daffodils, the itch of wool, the constraint of the boots marked the end of her childhood and freedom from responsibility and the beginning of a long and painful process of growing up. That earnest girl was I.

Somewhere in the Portland Street house there is a box of photographs, more than a century old, of Mother's earliest years. Myrna thinks where it might be, perhaps in the trunk in the spare bedroom.

Her mother had been a beautiful baby, with enormous and lively brown eyes, much loved and much photographed by her doting parents. Myrna recalls one faded photograph in particular, of baby Sidney seated in her pram, wearing a bonnet against the tropical sun. Standing behind the pram is a smiling black woman, perhaps the nanny. The railing of the verandah serves as a backdrop, and beyond is the blurry shape of mountains, their focus compromised by the limitations of the early camera. Soon after the photograph was taken came the twins, Daisy and Poppy, Myrna recalls, and some years later, her namesake aunt, little Myrna.

She thinks of young Sidney, her mother, and her little sisters running barefoot among the palms, and as babies, pacified by chewing on sugar cane. Not one of them kept their teeth beyond their twenties, but what contented, fat babies they must have been.

Hundreds of times Myrna has tried to imagine what it must have been like for the four girls to have been removed so suddenly from Paradise at such a young age, and taken by steamer during the soft March rains to the raw cold of London with no explanation, bribed into silence by their mother. "Ask me no questions and I'll paint your fingernails," she told them as the ship rolled on wintry seas, and the four girls complied, the lure of painted fingernails far more compelling than the truth about their philandering father. What comfort the four silhouettes hidden in Sidney's trunk must have been to the young girls, shadows of their childhood drawn only the Christmas previous by the father they left behind.

Their arrival in a wet, cold London must have been a dreadful shock, much as her own arrival in this place was, after leaving her own quiet Paradise on Portland Street.

How Myrna misses her kitchen with the sunlight streaming through the lace curtains, the red-and-white linoleum tiled floor, her apron hanging from a nail by the door and everything in its place. There was always something bubbling on the stove, a cake to be pulled from the oven, flowers to admire in the garden while she stood at the sink, gazing out the window while washing up. She misses the satisfaction of having cleaned and tidied the house, readying it for Frank's return from the high school where he taught, and in later years, the freedom of moving quietly about the place, stopping in the rooms of her choosing so she might enjoy fond memories.

Perhaps this morning she will go to the beauty parlour downstairs and have her fingernails painted.

᷿

There are three women seated in a row on molded plastic chairs, their heads covered with bulbous hair driers under which their thinning hair is hardening around curlers. One of them is reading a magazine, while the other two stare at nothing through droopy-lidded, milky eyes. There is a defeated look about them; the creases and folds of their faces sag and their necks refuse to straighten. Their time at the beauty parlour seems to have done little to improve their mood or appearance, in spite of Sally's best efforts. Myrna hopes she will be in a better state after her manicure. She fills her lungs with hairspray and nail polish fumes, tries not to cough.

"You have lovely hands, Mrs. Willoughby," says Sally, as she paints the second coat of Pearl-Pink onto Myrna's fingernails. It is nice to have her hand held by someone.

"My goodness, no, these are gardening hands," Myrna replies, surprised by Sally's words. She has always found her fingers too long, and now her knuckles are growing to look like walnuts.

"Well, they're certainly strong like a gardener's, but delicate like a florist's."

Myrna is moved by Sally's earnestness.

"Did you keep a garden before?" Sally looks up from her task. Her eyes are an unusual shade of green, like beach glass.

"I tried to keep up what my mother started in the Thirties, but of course back then they had a gardener. I had to let some things go." Myrna sighs.

"Yeah, well, gardening is hard work, isn't it? Personally, I keep a cherry tomato plant on the balcony, and a few geraniums in a pot. It's tough when you live in an apartment. They don't get a whole lot of sun."

Myrna nods and wonders how many daffodils are growing in the back yard this year. There must be scads of crocus under the maple, and the snowdrops should be nearly finished. Soon the forsythia hedge will bloom, and then the peonies along the back fence will push their buds out on lanky stems, beckoning the ants to come and open them, releasing the froth of pink blossoms. How she misses the assault of fragrance through the growing season, sitting on the verandah and breathing in the magnolia, the lilac, lily-of-the-valley. She misses too the freedom to stroll around the block, arm-in-arm with Frank on damp July evenings when the air was thick with the scent of linden.

There is so much that she misses. But there is no point in dwelling on it. Myrna tucks away her longing and turns her attention to her drying fingernails, pink as peonies.

"There you go, Mrs. Willoughby. Nice and shiny."

"Thank you, Sally. They're very cheerful on a cold March day."

Myrna feels buoyed by her shiny fingernails. Perhaps she will put on Mother's cocktail ring before going down to dinner.

∂

The amethyst shimmers in her hand. Even the fluorescent light in her room can't dull the sparkles caught in the facets of the stone. Such a simple design, silver vines with tiny leaves holding the stone in place. A ring fit for a gardener and a lady. Father gave it to Mother one Christmas, and Mother wore it every Saturday night to their dinners at the yacht club. It was the last thing she put on after buttoning up her dress, pulling on her seamed stockings, and slipping her feet into black patent leather heels. Mother loved the ring, and she took every opportunity to show it off.

"Crown jewels, my dear," she would say gaily, fluttering the fingers of her right hand so the stone would twinkle. "Some day it will be yours," words whose meaning always left a cold spike of dread lodged in the pit of young Myrna's stomach.

Myrna slips the ring on her finger past the first knuckle. When it wedges against the second knuckle she twists it until it eases past and into place. How pretty it looks with her pink fingernails; it will be something to show the ladies at her supper table, something new to talk about, a change from the usual gossip.

But she is disappointed by their reactions. Mrs. Boudreau, who is nearly blind, makes a polite noise, and stares off into the distance. Mrs. Ryan, whose husband died in the war, leaving her to raise her four children on her own, is

Binnie Brennan

unimpressed. And Miss MacMillan, who can never leave the matter of food for very long, simply changes the subject. Apparently the debate about rice pudding versus grape Jell-O is far more interesting than Myrna's beautiful ring.

Myrna turns the ring so the stone faces inside the palm of her hand. Now it is nothing more than a simple silver band, nothing special at all. She folds her right hand inside her left, and places them on her lap. When the girl brings around her dessert, she shakes her head no. Miss MacMillan offers to relieve her of her rice pudding.

࿔

"Well, the offer is just about finalized," says Peter, as he sits on the bed. "We've decided to put some of the furniture in storage." He is choosing his words carefully, Myrna can tell by the furrow between his eyebrows. "For now, anyway."

For now means until she dies, she knows this. The thought surprises Myrna in its matter-of-factness, the way the observation has simply popped into her head in the same way a glance out the window might tell her it's raining outside. But she has heard of this, in terms both bitter and resigned from fellow residents; dining-room talk of how the family is holding a yard sale, giving away to charity, or putting things in storage. She has heard it all. *We are our own best audience*, Myrna thinks, another thought which surprises her. But it is true: no matter what else she may think of this place and the people living here, it is a real democracy. They are all near the end of their lives, and the end of a tidy life isn't always itself tidy. *For now* will

84

allow her family a semblance of order while they pack up her home on Portland Street. Her life put away in boxes.

"Is there anything you'd like to have, Mother? From the house?"

He has always been a thoughtful boy. Myrna thinks of the four silhouettes, shadows of her mother and aunts drawn so long ago. They would look well above her bed.

"Why, yes, dear. I wouldn't mind having the silhouettes, if it's no trouble."

"Of course it's no trouble."

Peter's answer comes in a rush of what? Relief? Annoyance? The deepening furrow between his eyes could mean anything. Maybe he is simply tired.

"You look as though you could use a nap, dear," Myrna says carefully. Peter's face softens as he pushes back his hair. There is a sudden brilliance to his eyes.

"It's just that there's…" His voice catches, and his eyes squeeze shut. *Oh my*, Myrna thinks. *He is crying, my boy is crying.*

"Peter, dear?"

"Sorry, Mother," Peter runs a hand across his face, breathes in a wet-sounding rush. "Ahhh, wow! Did not expect that. Sorry."

Myrna reaches across and dabs his cheeks with her lace handkerchief.

"There must be an awful lot to do," she says. Peter simply nods and takes sudden, noisy breaths. "Don't trouble yourself with the silhouettes just now, dear. I'll remind you when the time comes." She would also like to have Mother's crystal stem vase, but that too can wait.

"I just feel so guilty, Mummy, about the house." Fresh tears ooze from his eyes, and he brings his hands together in a triangle, covering his nose and mouth. Myrna bites her lip. He has not called her Mummy in forty years.

"Peter, dear, there's no need for guilt. It's simply another phase in life, yours and mine. Think how happy you and Elizabeth will be in your new place. And think how contented I am here."

"You are?" Peter looks genuinely shocked. Myrna herself is surprised by her words. She thinks of Sally's kindness in the beauty parlour, and of the three old ladies sitting under hair driers, making the effort. Of the women with whom she shares her meals; the company they provide one another three times a day. And of course there's Nurse Muriel, with her colourful lips and happy chatter, always ready to listen, always willing to help. There is nothing like this for her on Portland Street.

"I am," she says with finality. It may not be the same thing as happiness, but Myrna is well looked-after and in the company of good people. Her son loves her. "Yes, I am very contented."

Peter blows a sigh of relief through his lips and covers her hand with his. It is broad, with sturdy knuckles, and his fingers quiver, then settle.

ॐ

The ring won't come off. It's not that her finger is fat; her knuckle must have swelled in the night.

"Knock-knock, good morning, Myrna." Nurse Muriel

peers around the door, beaming as always. Today her lips are pink and her hair is orange. "Fresh towels from Housekeeping. Thought I'd save them the trip since I was coming to see you anyways. How are you this morning?"

"Fine, thank you, except my ring won't come off."

Muriel sits on the bed across from her, and puts down the towels and the medications tray. She takes Myrna's hand and gently tugs at the ring.

"My golly, that's stuck, all right. Lemme get some soap and water. Won't be a tick."

Myrna stares at the ring while Nurse Muriel fills a bowl, brings the soap.

"Let's just soak your hand a minute in some cold water. It's a pretty ring, Myrna. Did your hubby give it to you?"

"It was my mother's. It's an amethyst, her birthstone."

"Well, it's beautiful. Sorry about your knuckle. Is it painful?"

"Not too bad, just a little swollen today."

"Cold water oughta help. Let's soap it up a bit and see what we can do, here. Pretty nail polish, is that Pearl-Pink?"

"Why, yes it is." Myrna is amazed. "How did you know?"

"Oh, I make it my business to know about these things. Like I say to my George, d'you think this just happens?" Muriel points at her lips and hair, and flutters her eyelashes. Then she gently twists the ring against Myrna's knuckle.

"I hope your George tells you how pretty you are."

Nurse Muriel throws her head back and laughs.

"The only thing my George tells me is who's ahead in the poker game at the Legion." The pressure against Myrna's knuckle is becoming painful. "And it's usually him, I tell ya. Whoopsie-daisy, off!"

Nurse Muriel holds up the ring, her eyes bright with triumph.

"Thank you, Nurse."

Muriel gently places the ring in Myrna's palm, and gathers her fingers around it. Muriel's own fingers are tipped with sparkling mauve.

"Oh, please. Call me Muriel, we're old friends. Listen, you could wear it around your neck on a chain, if you'd like, until that knuckle settles down."

"Oh, I don't think so. I wouldn't be able to admire it, would I? But thank you for your help, Muriel." Myrna knows the knuckle will not shrink, that her days of wearing Mother's ring are over.

"My pleasure. Is your son coming in to see you today?"

"Yes, he has a few things to bring over from the house. They're selling it, you know. It's been in the family since 1931." Myrna cannot help herself; she must speak of her loss.

"My goodness, that's a long time! I'll bet you've got a lot of happy memories."

"Yes, yes, I do. A lifetime of memories."

"Your son – Peter, isn't it? How's he feel about it?'

"Peter feels…" Myrna searches for the words, "Mixed feelings, I'd say."

Unexpected tears burn her eyelids, and she looks away, out the window and across the harbour. Beyond the Coast Guard mooring and on the other side of the hill is Portland Street. The pillared verandah steps of Mother's home fan down to the walkway and the green, green lawn, flanked by yew bushes trimmed to a perfect straight edge. A magnolia sprawls before the house, planted by Mother the year Peter was born. Every spring it leads the parade of blossoms, pale stars from which sweet fragrance wafts through the screen door, even with the late winter chill haunting the night air.

Most likely the yews are in need of pruning. The lawn will have burnt patches from the neighbours' dogs, likely the closest thing to fertilizer the grass has seen in years, Myrna is certain. Pounded into the lawn outside the stone wall there is a For Sale sign which soon will have a red slash across it, *Sold*. The house is hers no longer. And it has not been, really, not since she came here.

"How about I come by later and see what treasures Peter brings you? And listen, Mrs. Nickerson's family brought in some lovely daffodils for the nurses this morning. I'll put a few in a glass for you."

Daffodils. Nurse Muriel is so kind. Unable to speak, Myrna nods and forces a smile.

"Oops, I almost forgot why I came by in the first place. Here's your blood pressure pill, dear. There you go, drink up." Nurse Muriel watches while she washes down the pill and tosses the little paper cup in the waste basket.

ॐ

The late afternoon sun spills across Mother's diary, which sits on her desk, unopened. The photographs of her four grandchildren lie stacked on her bed. Myrna will have Peter find a place for them in her closet, and hang the four silhouettes on the waiting hooks in the wall. It will be a comfort to have them there.

She sits quietly on the wingback chair, looking out the window at the harbour. There is enough wind today to ruffle the water and push along a few sailboats in the far distance. Two ferries approach one another, blue-and-white ovals headed one to Halifax and the other to Dartmouth. In thirty minutes they will pass each other again, going in the opposite direction.

In Myrna's closed hand warms her mother's amethyst. Peter will be shocked when she gives it to him, and Elizabeth will be even more astounded. Whether or not Elizabeth chooses to wear it is anyone's guess; she can pass it on to one of the girls, if she wishes.

Myrna reaches for the diary and opens it to a page marked by a slip of paper, her mother's spring bulbs list of 1933. There are more than a hundred bulbs in total, costing eight dollars and twenty cents.

*May 1*st*, 1933*

First real day's work in the garden for me. I made a fence of sticks and string around the early tulip and Emperor daffodil bed, then I dug and tidied and de-rocked it. The cold edge was gone from the wind and the sun was shining gloriously.

Six

The clatter of the passing laundry cart is an invisible sound, almost unnoticeable, much as the feel of the wheelchair beneath her hands is nearly without sensation. Many hundreds, perhaps thousands of times Estella has pushed a wheelchair along this same dreary hallway, watching the polished floor tiles disappear one after another beneath the feet of the chair's occupant while she thinks ahead to what still needs to be done. For there is always someone waiting, someone who needs her, whether it be for a bath or meds or TV hour in the lounge. There is always something.

> *When the clouds hang heavy and it looks like rain,*
> *O Lord, how long?*

She stops at Mr. Walters' door and clips the brakes in place. The foot rests clang as she flips them out of harm's way.

Out of habit she draws a slow, searching breath. But for the usual counterpoint of old age, Javex and today's lunch, the air is calm.

Mr. Walters is easy; he is slight and docile, even polite. With a firm hand she guides him from his recliner, helps him turn in tiny steps, and waits while his shaking, gnarled hand reaches behind for the safety of the arm rest. The moment of seating is accomplished with a gust of stale air. He lifts one foot and then the other for her to place on the foot rests. Then Mr. Walters smiles, nodding slightly. He does not look at her. Estella saves her own smile for another time.

Nurse Muriel looks up from her seat at the nursing station as Estella wheels Mr. Walters past.

"Looking handsome tonight, Mr. W.! Got a date for *Wheel of Fortune*?" Her voice rattles down the hallway, chasing after them. Mr. Walters chuckles and waves, nodding his head. Looks right at Muriel the whole time. Estella keeps going, thinking ahead to the med cart records, which need checking before bedtime rounds.

She knows they assume things about her, these old people who know no better than what their parents told them, nearly a hundred years ago. Old fears ill-founded in the first place, but transcending time: *Wouldn't dare sit on the same trolley, now, would you?*

Some of it she has heard them say aloud: *Tall girl like you must have been a basketball player in your day.*

Estella has never in her life touched a basketball.

She lets them assume. There was a time when she hated them for it, but now she hides behind their fears and assumptions. Her job at the nursing home, awful though it can be, provides her with what she needs to help her daughter along.

This she reminds herself during the times when she despairs of assisting on one more bath, of wiping one more elderly, white behind. Of listening to Muriel's incessant chatter, all that silly noise about her husband, her mother, and the cute new fellah, Sam the nurses' aide.

Muriel's voice cuts through her like a knife. She gets her name wrong every time. But that's fine by Estella. She is happy to keep herself apart from this place.

"Here you go, Mr. Walters. Just in time."

She lines up his chair next to Mrs. Nickerson, who half-turns and smiles, her wrinkled face expectant as the theme song to *Wheel of Fortune* begins.

૭

I sing because I'm happy
I sing because I'm free
For His eye is on the sparrow
And I know He watches me

What nobody knows about Estella is that come Sunday morning, she is transformed. Nobody knows because nobody asks.

The day always begins early, Estella awake before the birds, washing and scrubbing, the better to worship later. Once the floors are done, the kitchen sink and the stovetop gleaming,

Estella turns to the crisp white blouse, ironed and laid out with her blue skirt and jacket, nipped at the waist with a small flare in back. As she slides her feet into shiny black slingbacks, a shiver runs straight up from her toes to the back of her neck, and when she dons her matching blue hat, broad-brimmed and with its navy silk ribbon, she knows she's ready to receive her Lord Jesus.

The walk to Cherrybrook Baptist Church fills her with goodness. With long strides and her head held high, Estella prepares. Humming quietly at first, by the time she takes her place in the choir stall her voice is ready to swoop and swirl.

Reverend Earl knows not to keep her waiting, so he makes his announcements brief before launching into his sermon. He has long known that Estella is his partner, that his sermons are not merely ornamented, but completed by her voice. Sunday after Sunday his signal to her remains unchanged. He revs her like an engine, calling to his flock, bringing them in with talk and rhythm until finally he shouts to Jesus, and in an explosion worthy of Armageddon Estella throws back her head and, her body swaying and her hands fluttering, she howls the Gospel with the angels themselves.

꙰

Stony the road we trod, bitter the chast'ning rod
Felt in the days when hope unborn has died
Yet with a steady beat, have not our weary feet
Come to the place for which our fathers sighed?

The woman standing before the nursing station is distraught beyond words. She tries to speak, and tries again without success. In anguish, she buries her face in the roses she is carrying. It is her first time back since her father died. Estella's thoughts click into place: Mr. Jeffreys, late last week, room 427. Stroke. No, heart, taken mercifully in his sleep. This is his daughter, Amanda.

"It's nice to see you, Amanda," she says carefully.

"I…I just wanted to thank you nurses for all you've done for us. Years ago Daddy planted a wild rose bush in our front yard…." The woman closes her eyes. Breathes deeply. "It was for their silver wedding anniversary." She cannot continue.

"Why don't I put those in water?" Estella reaches for the flowers. "I'll leave them right here for everyone to enjoy."

Amanda nods and turns to the elevator. Her sadness works like gravity, pulling at her shoulders. Time will help, Estella knows, but she will not say so out loud. It's not her place. She stands watching as the newly fatherless daughter steps into the elevator. Presses the button. Manages a small wave.

Wild rose means love, means innocence. It also means loss. The peppery-sweet scent casts Estella's thoughts back to the windy shores of her childhood, filled with family, the Gospel, sisters, brothers, and elders all living in the home built by her grandfather on the lip of the Atlantic.

When the bulldozers came to tear down the town, her father combed his hair and dressed in his Sunday finest. Then he chained himself to the family home.

❧

Papa was her hero, always. Tall, strong, impeccably dressed, with a crease like a knife edge along his pant legs, Estella's father was firm in his convictions, with a strength that made itself clear with the back of his massive hand when one or another of the children misbehaved. Estella kept out of trouble by spending her days humming, and when she knew he was around, she raised her voice to within his ears' reach in hopes of winning a rare smile. A church deacon possessed of the strongest basso voice in the choir, Papa encouraged Estella's singing. Such a talent was a great responsibility, and he declared that singing the Gospel would be her mission. A girl would never preach. But she could sing the Word so the world might listen.

Every Sunday after church, Papa would sit her on his knee, and the two of them listened to the radio, symphony concerts from Toronto, opera from New York. When it was over he'd say the same thing, week after week: "Those musicians are touching the toe of God, Estella, just like you do every time you sing. Sweet Jesus." Then he'd ease her to the floor, and she'd run off to find her sister Irene, wondering all the while about God's toe.

Estella was tiny and her hair still in braids when Duke Ellington passed through Africville. Her father carried her to the front of the crowd and had her sing *Lift Every Voice and Sing*. She planted her small feet on the ground and breathed the air in and pushed the words out so Jesus above might hear them. Mr. Ellington, suave in his pinstripe and his pencil moustache, squinted and smiled through a cloud of cigarette smoke. He nodded his Brylcremed head, giving his blessing.

Later that night, she and her sister sneaked through the orchard to the tavern and listened to Mr. Ellington and his band play. The rhythm filled the salt air and Estella's soul, and she closed her eyes and swayed in the darkness, consumed by the richness of the blues, the colours of jazz, the scent of rose flowing around her. Their drunken older brother, Roy, discovered the sisters shivering in the bushes when he came outside to take a leak. He cuffed them both, but dragged only Irene back to their home, leaving Estella to listen and learn.

The rattling of the laundry cart startles her.

"Nice flowers, Estella. Need a vase?"

"No thanks, Sam. I think there's one in the staff room."

౨

Remember me, forget my fate

"Lovely day, isn't it?"

"Lovely, yes."

Estella is in too great a hurry to address the matter of the fog blanketing the harbour outside the lounge window. Nor does she register who has spoken the predictable words. A blue perm flattened by sleep, gaudy pink lipstick, and a pale cardigan are all she takes in as she rushes to her next task. It could be one of ten residents Estella can think of, but she must move on. The sores on Mr. Walters' legs took longer than usual to clean and bandage, and Miss Crenshaw will be waiting for her bath.

Her pace slows outside room 427. The door is slightly ajar, and the sound of singing curls its way around it and fills the antiseptic hallway. For a moment the clatter of carts and the barking of laughter from the nursing station fade while Estella stands still with her eyes closed. It is a Purcell aria, she is certain, from the opera *Dido and Aeneas*. The soprano reaches the moment of heartbreak, singing the words with such purity that Estella can't breathe. Sweet Jesus, she must listen to the end.

When the last note fades into the everyday racket of this place, Estella exhales. She runs a quick hand across her eyes and continues along the hallway she has traversed a thousand times. The floor looks dull, in need of polishing.

෭

I live in a big city
And they tell me that we are free
Now I hear these babies cryin'
Do you know what that's doin' to me?

When finally the police came, Estella's father was weeping and ranting for his father's home, his grandfather's freedom, for Jesus' sacrifice. The sheriff cut his chains, and, looking no-one in the eye, he and two policemen dragged him off to the waiting paddywagon. The town's women stood side by side, holding brightly coloured hats to their heads as the wind whipped their jeers and catcalls around the receding quartet. While the law enforcers stared at the ground, their faces grim,

Estella's father held his head high, his face slick with tears.

Hidden in the branches of a nearby apple tree, Estella and Irene watched. While Irene whimpered and rubbed at her eyes, a scream lodged in the back of Estella's throat, waiting for release. But instead, when the wagon pulled away taking her Papa from her, Estella lifted her voice and sang.

᷇

Sometimes I'm up, sometimes I'm down
O yes, Lord
Sometimes I'm almost on de groun'
O yes, Lord

"Stella, honey, would you give me an assist in 427? Mrs. Nickerson has a hair appointment."

Estella nods, sloshes out the bedpan, and joins Muriel.

"Hellooo, Mrs. Nickerson!"

Muriel's voice rattles around in Estella's ears. Mrs. Nickerson glances at her with pale eyes dulled by meds and then speaks to Muriel.

"It's just that I can't get up on my own today, and I have a hair appointment. My daughter's coming to lunch, you see. Her name is Sarah."

"That's okay, dear. Stella and I can help you into your wheelchair."

While Muriel is speaking, Estella readies the chair, clipping the brakes, steadying herself on the old woman's left. Mrs. Nickerson gives her a tentative look as Estella places one hand under her forearm and the other around her shoulder. Estella knows the look well, and she reminds herself that, ill-founded or not, the old woman's fear is real. Ever so slightly she lightens her touch on Mrs. Nickerson's arm.

"Here we go, dear, on three. Whoopsie-daisy, three!"

Will Muriel ever shut up?

"I'll wheel you over to the elevator, Mrs. Nickerson. Sam can take you down to the hairdresser. Sam, or *Sam*-ee! Here he is, dear. Handsome, isn't he? You have yourself a nice lunch with your daughter."

Estella thinks of Irene, her own daughter, and smiles inwardly.

❧

We shall overcome, some day

We all have our way of touching God's toe, Estella has told her daughter from the beginning.

Abidemi, named for Estella's sister Irene until her recent epiphany on the shores of West Africa, is close to finishing her degree in law school. With her braids tied artfully or covered in a brilliant headwrap, depending on her mood and purpose, Abidemi is bulldozing her way to justice. Driven by legend, Abidemi will see to it that men like her grandfather never again need chain themselves to what belongs to them and that boys such as her brother, LeRoy, might pull themselves out of the welfare loop and begin to take themselves seriously. Demand they be *taken* seriously.

By the age of ten, Estella's daughter could recite Dr. King's freedom speeches, and she regularly lectured her classmates on the virtues of non-violent protest. This didn't go over well with her peers, bussed as they were to an affluent neighbourhood where they were never really welcomed. Abidemi, then Irene, didn't have many friends. But her anger fuelled her success and she excelled in school, won scholarships through university, and is now working her lonely way through law school.

Estella knows that pride is a sin. But occasionally she wraps herself in it, revelling in her daughter's ambition. She wears her pride secretly like a mink stole. Then she quietly goes about her work, saving every penny to help pay her daughter's way. Her own anger she has learned to keep safe, channeling it in the only useful way she knows how.

☙

Darkness shades me

Someone is dying.

Mingled with the scent of medication, starchy food, and floor polish hangs the fragrance of death. Miss Crenshaw's bath will have to wait.

As Estella rushes past the nursing station, Sam stops her with a hand on her arm.

"It's Mrs. Nickerson. She stroked out at the hairdresser. It'll be quick, if she's not already gone."

Estella nods and takes quick strides to room 427. She pulls up the chair and holds the old woman's hand. Watches her still, white face, her concave chest rising in short gasps. "Dido's Lament" comes to Estella.

> *More I would, but death invades me*
> *Death is now a welcome guest*

Soon the family will arrive. Estella will give them their time, if only Mrs. Nickerson will breathe a little longer.

> *When I am laid in earth*
> *May my wrongs create no trouble in thy breast*

Estella enfolds the cooling hand in hers, massages it, and lets the words wash over them both.

> *Remember me, but ah! forget my fate*

The door has opened, and the son enters with halting steps. His wife rushes past him and stops at the foot of the bed. With frightened eyes she looks first at her mother-in-law, then at Estella for some kind of reassurance.

"She's still with us," Estella says softly. "Why don't you sit with her, hold her hand?"

On her way out Estella pulls at the door to keep their choked goodbyes private. The door remains slightly ajar, as usual. Estella looks down the hall, sees Muriel's rounded behind as she enters the staff room. There is no-one around to disturb the family. Estella leaves 427 and walks slowly, her steps measured in even breaths.

ॐ

Yes, when this flesh and heart shall fail
And mortal life shall cease
I shall possess within the veil
A life of joy and peace

Mrs. Nickerson's death has left Muriel a wet and sobbing mess. Estella finds her sitting in the staff room, weeping into a tissue, her ample bosom heaving with sighs of loss. She pours a coffee, stirring in cream and extra sugar, and places it by Muriel's elbow. Sips her own and waits.

This is always the way with Muriel. She takes the deaths hard, has a good cry in the privacy of the staff room, and then washes her face and brightly goes about the business of helping the living. The two of them have been working together for so long, Estella knows not to say anything.

"I know you sat with her, Stella." Muriel's voice is rough from crying.

Estella nods, "A person shouldn't die alone."

"I was outside the room, waiting."

Estella says nothing, but stares into her Styrofoam cup.

"Our shift was nearly over. I thought I might spell you." Muriel dabs at the corners of her eyes in a futile effort not to smudge her mascara, which is already running in dark rivers over the mounds of her cheeks. "So I pulled up a chair. The door was open a crack. You know, 427 never really closes properly."

Estella's jaw tightens. The moments she spends at the end of a resident's life are precious, a private matter between herself and the dying.

"Stella, you were singing. I...." This time Muriel blots, then wipes her eyes. Estella looks away. "You have such a beautiful voice, I had no idea. In all the years we've worked shifts together, I've never heard you so much as hum a tune."

"I just like to sing them a prayer," Estella murmurs. "Help them on their way."

"I never knew." Muriel's voice is for once quiet, thoughtful.

                                                   ≈

Let our rejoicing rise, high as the list'ning skies
Let it resound loud as the rolling sea

There is another thing nobody knows about Estella.

Come Friday nights she is again transformed. From her tall, angular self, with her wide-set, stern eyes and pointed cheekbones, she emerges a glittering creature of the night. Sliding into her shiny black slingbacks, Estella welcomes the familiar shiver of anticipation. Shimmering in a blue strapless gown, which clings to her like mist, earrings dangling beneath her full, curly wig, Estella steps out of the taxi and hurries, humming, through the back door to Foxxie's Tavern.

Walter Foxx, the owner, knows that she is his partner in Friday night's success. He agrees to no strippers on Fridays, and he pays her a percentage of the cover, plus tips. She always delivers: Estella is worth her weight in gold to him.

Walter keeps her waiting offstage for only so long, seducing his audience with tales of Estella's exotic past, of how she once sang in made-up Parisian music halls and lived among princes and sheikhs, while in the shadows of the wings she clutches the microphone in her sweaty hand and quivers. With Walter's same words every time, *"I bring you Estella, Star of the Night!"* Estella strides onstage and brings the microphone to her shiny red lips, her head thrown back and her body shuddering. Her hands flutter in the lights as, dodging God's toe, she moans and shrieks out the blues.

Acknowledgements

The diary entries in Chapter 5 are drawn verbatim from the 1932 gardening diary of Sidney Carmen Payzant (née Shaw), my late grandmother.

Many thanks to the elders in my life for their grace, wit and wisdom; and to family and friends who read the novella in its early days. Infinite gratitude to my circle of writers: Renee Hartleib, Erna Buffie, Janice Acton, Judy Adamson, Michelle Mulder, and Mary Keenan, without whose perspective I would have left out far too much.

For his careful and honest guidance in the later stages I am indebted to MG Vassanji.

The staff at the Northwood Centre in Halifax and the Toronto Grace Hospital, by their quiet and effective work, were a source of inspiration. I thank also Sandra Witherbee for her insights into the nursing profession, and Jo Brennan for her courage.

Thanks, too, to the Nova Scotia Department of Tourism, Culture and Heritage for its generous assistance; and to the Writers' Federation of Nova Scotia, the Humber School for Writers, and Symphony Nova Scotia.

I am grateful to Quattro Books for their belief in this work, and to Sheree Fitch, Parker Duchemin, and Carol Bruneau for the same.

Most of all, to Tim, Tamsyn and Avery: I thank you.

Song Lyrics

"O Lord, How Long?" (Traditional)
"His Eye Is on the Sparrow" by Charles H. Gabriel
"Lift Every Voice and Sing" by John Rosamond Johnson
"Dido's Lament" by Henry Purcell
"Big City Blues" by Big Maceo Merriweather
"Nobody Knows" by Henry Thacker Burleigh
"We Shall Overcome" by Rev. Charles Tindley
"Amazing Grace" by John Newton

Marquis Book Printing Inc.

Québec, Canada
2009